"Just drop that Winchester and
turn around with some stars
in your hands, friend . . ."

The other man did no such thing. So Stringer shot
him before he could swing the muzzle of that
Winchester far enough to worry more about, and
the rifle ball pitchforked its human target sideways into the campfire. As Stringer rose he expected to see the cuss at least try to roll off the hot
coals. But he didn't.

Stringer swore and scooped up the nearby coffeepot to pour over the sprawled man. The coffee
was still hot, but he didn't seem to mind, and it
kept his shirt from burning off entirely. Stringer
kicked the fire higher to have a look at what he'd
just done. He could see at a glance the rascal was
stone dead as well as toasted.

LOU CAMERON

STRINGER

ON DEAD MAN'S RANGE

CHARTER BOOKS, NEW YORK

STRINGER ON DEAD MAN'S RANGE

A Charter Book / published by arrangement with
the author

PRINTING HISTORY
Charter edition / September 1987

ISBN: 0-441-79022-4

Charter Books are published by The Berkley Publishing Group,
200 Madison Avenue, New York, New York 10016.
The name "Charter" and the "C" logo are trademarks
belonging to Charter Communications, Inc.
PRINTED IN THE UNITED STATES OF AMERICA

10 9 8 7 6 5 4 3 2 1

CHAPTER
ONE

It was one of those rare and lovely mornings when the Frisco Bay lay Caribbean blue under a smiling cloudless sky. But there was no joy in the press room of the *San Francisco Sun*. The feature editor, Swearing Sam Barca, was carrying on in a manner that threatened the frosted glass of his corner cubicle and had just caused the society editor working fifty feet away to insert an obscenity that hardly belonged in the wedding announcement he was trying to type up.

Inside the glass box the object of Swearing Sam's wrath was calmly rolling a Bull Durham smoke as he waited for the storm to let up. Swearing Sam Barca was short, dark, and ugly. The target of his editorial integrity was living proof that while one could take a cowhand off the range, it was harder to take the range out of the cowhand. Stuart MacKail, ace stringer for the *Sun,* was a lot taller, less dark, and a lot prettier than the ferocious little Sicilian swearing at him. He was dressed as city-slicker as the business district of the city by the bay required since the vigilantes had cleaned up the nearby Barbary Coast. But he still looked as if he was ready to fork a bronc and ride, if he had to. He'd worked his way through Stanford working stock for a local cattle spread.

As he licked the neatly wrapped tan paper to seal it, the man on the far side of the feature desk snapped, "Don't you dare light that infernal cornhusk in here. It would stink bad enough if I had a window to open. Why can't you smoke cigars or, hell, tailor mades like everyone else?"

Stringer, as they called him half in admiration and half in jest, said, "At the space rates you pay me, I'm lucky to be able to afford any tobacco at all. Could we get back to the feature you seem so upset about? There's not a word I turned in that I can't document, Sam."

Barca rolled his eyes heavenward to stare at the pressed-tin ceiling through his green eyeshade as he groaned, "Oh, Jesus H. Christ, here we go with that insane notion that the truth and the news are the same thing!" He pointed a bony finger at Stringer and thundered, "Not a one of those heathen Chinee along Grant Avenue subscribe to the *San Francisco Sun*. Those who do, in considerable numbers, consider Chinatown a blight on prime real estate as well as a disgrace to their fair city!"

Stringer struck a match head afire with a horny thumbnail and lit his smoke before he said, "That's the point of my expose, Sam. The machinations of certain real estate interests to move Chinatown down to the mud flats near Hunter's Point are a short-sighted attempt to make things disgusting for every-body. You don't have to admire chop suey or give a damn about them who cooks it to see that any kind of shantytown on them mud flats will ruin those flats for the shrimp and oysters now gathered there in considerable numbers for the enjoyment of Frisco folk who hate Chinese cooking. This town was built by the bay because the bay made it a good place to be. What's the sense of building a city by a bay if quick-buck rascals are allowed to fill said-bay in?"

Old Sam looked wistful despite himself, and replied, "I used to buy a whole bag of them bitty shrimp for a nickel when I was young and foolish. There was this old chink who sold 'em off the hulk of a stranded schooner near the foot of Mission Street. He's gone now. The hulk he was squatting on would be a couple of blocks inland, if it's still there, under the railroad yards. I don't think I've ever enjoyed anything I could buy so cheap as I enjoyed them little popcorny shrimp on a raw day after school. But the developers who hate to see mud flats wasted on seafood advertise regular in our real estate section. Until such time as oyster tongers, clam diggers, and shrimp netters see fit to pay for space in this newspaper, we are not, repeat *not* going to run any features insulting those who do."

Stringer said, "Damn it, Sam. I was counting on the money for that piece."

Barca picked up a wire service dispatch from the mess atop his desk as he said, "Count again. I told you before, you'd do better if you waited for me to *assign* you a feature I could use instead of typing at windmills on your own. I got one here that ought to be right up your alley. The front office was pleased with that wild west shootout you just covered up in the Mother Lode."

Stringer protested, "Damn it, Sam. I wasn't old

enough to write up *anything* the year Billy the Kid
and Jesse James was both put in the box forever. This
is the twentieth century. I want to cover modern
times, not that wild west crap you so admire."

"You grew up in a mighty wild west, didn't you?"
growled the man who stood between Stringer and the
payment of his rent.

Stringer took a deep drag on his smoke to get his
own temper under control before he replied, "We
were doing our best to calm things down as I was
growing up in the Mother Lode cow country. Had I
wanted to stay that rustic, I'd have never worked my
way through college."

Barca smiled crookedly at him and said, "They
may have taught you to write, but you still talk like a
trail driver. As to how wild some parts of our modern
west might be, Butch and the Sundance Kid are still
at large, and have you read that new best-seller by
Owen Wister?"

Stringer nodded and said, "*The Virginian* is all
right, I reckon. But you have to go some today to
find parts of the west where things are still so informal."

Barca said, "I'm sending you to one. In Arizona
Territory. I have it on good authority that the tough
little cowtown of Holbrook Arizona was the site of
the original Bucket of Blood Saloon, and that fur-
thermore, said Bucket of Blood is still in business."

Stringer looked pained and said, "Hell, Sam, Holbrook ain't been wild in years. It was tamed years
ago by a firm but fair lawman whose name escapes
me."

Swearing Sam looked pleased with himself, and
said, "The man's name was, and still is, Commodore

Perry Owens. Commodore isn't a title. It's his Christian name. You would have been too young at the time to pay attention to distant range wars. But I wasn't. So I got to cover some of Perry's town taming as a reporter. He did have a way of taming towns. A lot of penny dreadfuls have since been written, based on his real adventures."

Stringer groaned and said, "I suspect I've read them. Not even you could be so cruel as to send me out in the field in summer to rehash gunfights old enough to vote, for God's sake!"

Barca nodded, but said, "I don't want too much on what Perry did in his glory days. Just a little background to show how ungrateful or forgetful the voters of Navajo County have just acted in their infinite wisdom."

Stringer raised a questioning eyebrow. So Barca nodded and continued, "They just voted him out of office—after all his years of service to a now much more civilized community. I want you to go find out why."

Stringer protested, "All the way to Arizona, in high summer? Surely you jest. It's a free country, Sam. Why can't the voters choose a new sheriff if they want one?"

Barca insisted, "The man they elected to replace Perry has no rep as a lawman. If we assume he kisses babies just swell, it's still sort of fishy. I've followed old Perry's career over the years since he commenced to risk his life for those ingrates, way back in '86. He may have bent the Constitution a few times as he strove to restore law and order to country too tough for Apache to mess with, but in all the years since, not one whiff of scandal or corruption ever stained his good name. He'd be in his early fifties now. That's way too young to send such a fine lawman out to pasture. I want to find out what really happened."

Stringer said, "You sound like you're taking his election loss sort of personal, Sam."

Barca replied, "I am. One night in the Bucket of Blood some uncouth Hash Knife riders took it in their heads to make a young wop reporter dance the Tarantella for them to the dulcet notes of their six-guns. Commodore Perry Owens made 'em stop and bought me a drink to steady my nerves. My teeth were still chattering, but he told me I'd acted like a man when I refused to dance, even with one boot tip shot off. I never forgot that, or him. If he was crooked out of his job, I mean to print an expose indeed. So what are you waiting for, a kiss good-bye?"

Stringer rose to his considerable height, but said, "Arizona is quite a walk from here, and I'm down to a modest jingle in these pants."

Barca thought a moment, then said, "I'll tell you what. I'll sign a voucher for that feature you wrote about the mud flats. I'm allowed to pay for stories we don't have space to run, if I don't overdo it. You go home and get packed, and by the time you get back they may have the check made out for you."

Stringer swore softer but no less dirty, and added, "Damn it, old hoss, that's my own money, not expense money we're speaking of so loosely!"

Barca shrugged and pointed out, "It's your own stubborn desire to work free-lance in the field that keeps you so broke, you know. If you'd take the staff job I've offered you, more than once, you wouldn't have to worry about travel expenses."

Stringer looked disgusted. "Have it your way," he said. "I'd eat all the mud off Hunter's Point, raw, before I'd risk getting old and ornery as you, chained to a fool desk."

Stringer was still feeling used and abused, but by the time he got to his boarding house on Rincon Hill, south of the Slot, he was less morose about the satanic pact he'd been forced to make with his goat-faced feature editor. Arizona Territory at this time of the year was hardly the place he'd have picked to spend a weekend in the country, even on someone else's money. But it would be good to get out of these sissy duds and prissy town for a spell.

As he climbed the stairs to his furnished digs under the mansard roof, he saw that the gal on the second landing was home from her night job as an artist's model at the school on Russian Hill. He nodded as politely as one could nod to a naked lady reclining on a brass bedstead with her door wide open. She blew a cloud of violet-scented tobacco smoke at him, saying, "I don't have an escort for the Artist's Ball this evening, Mr. MacKail."

He was trying to keep their boarding-house relationship formal as well. So he called her Miss as he explained he had to leave town before anything so interesting was likely to take place. He didn't know her real name. The title the other boarders had given her hardly went with Miss, even if it fit.

He hoped it didn't as he went on up to his lonely little room to change and pack. His grasshopper typewriter was too heavy and too antique to pack. He left it where it sat near the window and settled for a note-pad and a couple of extra pencils instead. The story

Sam Barca wanted didn't sound complicated, and as long as a reporter spelled all the names right, nobody fussed if he missed a detail here and there in shorthand.

Knowing Arizona in the summer, he packed a sheepskin against possibly cold desert nights, and a yellow rain slicker against the even more unlikely event of such an astounding event. He got out of his city duds and into a thinner well-broken-in, once blue-denim range outfit. He knotted a black sateen kerchief in place of the shoestring tie he'd just tossed over a bedpost, and stomped into his worn, soft, but still too-tight black Justins. They might have been easier to get into if he hadn't shrunk gunmetal spurs to them with soaked and stretched rawhide. But it made no sense to wear spurs that had any chance of coming loose at an awkward moment aboard a bronc. He considered his gun rig before he packed it in with the other possibles in his battered gladstone bag. He knew it wasn't considered civilized to wear a gun on the streets of Frisco these days. But even these days the bitty town of Holbrook was situated in a sort of uncivilized neck of the woods.

He tossed in some socks and a spare blue-collar work shirt and sat on the gladstone to lock it. Then he put on the once pearl-gray Rough Rider's hat he'd brought home from the Spanish American War and headed back down the stairs.

As he passed the open door of the gal on the second landing again, she called out, "You don't know what you'll be missing, cowboy."

He didn't answer. He had a pretty good idea what he was passing up each time he passed her door. For 'even if she didn't live up to that dreadful nickname they'd given her, he could see what *else* the shameless model had to offer. It was a wonder even the prissier art students managed to sketch half of those Junoesque curves without dropping their charcoal. He'd heard they carried on even wilder at those Artist's Balls, and that sure sounded a sight to see. But a man who messed with women where he worked or boarded was asking for a colder gray Monday morning than any Saturday night could be worth. So he managed to get back to the office as pure as he'd left.

When he did, the head bookkeeper who signed the checks was out to lunch and not expected back until after the banks shut their doors for the day. Swearing Sam Barca was sore about that too. He took Stringer aside and growled, "Don't you dare let this get around. But here's enough to make it to Holbrook, and I'll wire you a money order for that otherwise-useless exposé once you get there."

Without counting it, Stringer pocketed the wad of silver certificates the older man had slipped him. But he could tell that even if they were all singles, Swearing Sam had dug into his own pocket pretty deep. Stringer nodded and said, "I'll catch the next S.P. Coaster south and see if I can make connections with the eastbound Santa Fe this evening in L.A. You must be in one hell of a hurry to get me to Holbrook if you're paying for it so personal, Sam."

Barca nodded grimly and said, "I told you Sheriff Owens was an old drinking pal of mine. I want his side of the story, and if those damned Republicans screwed him out of his job by crooking the election, I mean to shout it from the rooftops in banner headlines!"

Stringer said that sounded fair, but added, "Correct me if I'm wrong, Sam, but ain't the *San Franciso Sun* owned by Republicans, with an editorial policy to match?"

Barca nodded. "It is. What of it? It's our duty to print the truth and let the chips fall where they may, right?"

Stringer frowned down at the peppery little Sicilian and said, "I thought you were trying to get me to drop that self-destructive notion, Sam."

Barca said, "This is different. Commodore Perry Owens is not a heathen Chinee. He's as good an American as you or me, even if he is a Democrat. So go find out how they screwed him, and let *me* do the fretting about editorial policy, damn it!"

CHAPTER
TWO

Navajo County was the name the Arizona Territory had finally settled on for about ten thousand square miles of its rougher range atop the Colorado Plateau. A good part of the vast county was in theory still run directly from Washington as Indian reserve or federal open range. Who got to run the rest of it had long been disputed with some heat by its sparse but noisy population of Indians, Mexicans, and Anglos of Mormon-Gentile-Sheep-Cattle-Yankee-Reb persuasion.

Until circa 1883 the President's appointed territorial governors had been content to let the locals work things out for themselves. Nobody socially acceptable seemed to be getting hurt, and at least the noise seemed to keep the Apache calm. But then the silvery rails of the Atchison, Topeka & The Santa Fe reached the Little Colorado, and since the Iron Horse had a ferocious thirst for boiler water, the railroaders built the jerkwater stop of Holbrook there. Most anywhere the Iron Horse stopped was a handy place to load beef on the hoof, and thus, to the surprise of the railroaders who'd thought they were crossing a desert just to get somewhere more important, a wild and woolly little cowtown had mushroomed into existence almost overnight.

The Bucket of Blood Saloon, one of the first services opened to cater to the needs of the cattle industry in Holbrook, was still in business near the railroad stop when Stringer climbed down from the coach car he'd ridden one hell of a ways to save on pocket money. He was stiff all over and his mouth tasted like the bottom of a garbage can after washing down all those stale sandwiches with the orange soda pop they allowed to be sold in the coach cars. So, first things coming first, Stringer toted his gladstone over to the Bucket of Blood, set it down on the sawdust near the brass foot rail running the length of the bar in lieu of seats, and told the kindly looking old gent behind the mahogany that he'd drink anything wet but might enjoy a cold beer even better.

The barkeep sighed and said, "The word cold is a matter of some discussion in these parts at this time of the year. I got some bottled Steamer in the ice chest, and the last time I looked a few shards of ice was left. Our draft is cheaper by far, but while it ain't quite warm enough to brew tea with, I feel it best to warn any man packing a gun that it's mighty warm."

Stringer chuckled and ante'd four bits on the bar between them as he said the Steamer sounded more like what he'd had in mind. A few moments later, as the older man poured mostly suds from a modest brown bottle, he sensed he'd been slickered again. But at least it was Steamer and it wasn't quite as warm as the rest of the brick kiln he seemed to be standing in at the moment.

As his eyes adjusted to the gloom of the dinky saloon after squinting at the glaring sunlight outside, Stringer saw there were a couple of other customers, seated at a corner table. They were both making every effort to avoid looking his way. So Stringer didn't look at them again as he told the barkeep, "I've come all this way from the coast to have a few words with your Sheriff Owens. You wouldn't happen to know where I could find him, would you?"

The barkeep proceeded to polish the already polished and otherwise vacant bar as he murmured, "Not hardly. He ain't anyone's sheriff no more, not since the last election. We do have a sheriff, though, and a town marshal as well. It's no business of mine, but I can't say either would be too pleased with that .45 you've got hanging on your hip, son."

Stringer smiled and said, "It's not a .45. It's a .38 service revolver I brought back from the war with Spain. I wear it openly because some lawmen find it even more unsettling to notice a gun-sized bulge under a stranger's duds. I don't know why a less open and aboveboard cuss might want to look your old sheriff up with evil intents, but since I can see you may have read me wrong, I'd best advise you I'm a harmless newspaper man. They call me Stringer MacKail. I ride for the *San Franciso Sun*. They sent me here to talk with old Commodore Perry Owens about that election he just managed to lose after seventeen years of service with so few complaints."

The barkeep shrugged and said, "I didn't vote for neither side. I'm a Socialist, and only the Democrats and Republicans ran anyone for County Sheriff. I ain't seen old Owens since he lost the election. I think they said he lived on a cow spread just outside of town with his family. I can't say just where it might be, though."

Stringer sensed the older man was more uneasy than ignorant. As he sipped some more beer he felt a slight draft on his cheek. He glanced at the entrance to see the bat-wings were still in swing on their hinges. He glanced at the mirror behind the barkeep and saw the two men seated in the corner had been the ones who'd just left. He didn't think anything of it until the anxious looking barkeep moved closer, leaned across the bar, and said, "That beer is on the house, son. Now do me a favor and take the bottle with you as you leave!"

Stringer raised a thoughtful eyebrow as he asked, "Are you trying to throw me out for some reason, friend?"

The older man shook his head and said, "I ain't about to try no such thing. I am a man of peace and social justice. It's been a spell since this saloon got named so deservingly, and I just want to keep it that way."

Stringer nodded and said, "I noticed those gents listening in seemed sort of moody. Am I just supposed to guess what I might have said to offend them, or would you like to give me a hint?"

The now ashen-faced barkeep shook his head and said, "I serve drinks, pretzels, and cold cuts across this bar. Nothing else. I run a saloon here, not an information service, savvy?"

Stringer said, "I'm starting to. Let's make a deal. You tell me where I can find Sheriff Owens, and I'll be on my way before those gents get back with whoever they went to get."

The old man might have told him, in time, had there been more time. But then the bat-wings swung again and a tall galoot wearing a cordovan charro outfit and a brace of Colt Lightings in a silver-mounted buscadero rig was standing there, scowling like he thought he was posing for the cover of a pulp magazine as he demanded, low and growly, to know who was so interested in the late Sheriff Commodore Perry Owens.

Stringer smiled pleasantly and said, "I hadn't heard he was late. I only heard he'd lost that last election. I take it he no longer resides in this fair city?"

The scowling gun slick said, "You take it right. I run him out of town myself."

Stringer's expression didn't change as he observed softly, "You must be good at running gents out of town, then."

The other man nodded grimly and said, "I am. I am known as Blue Streak Bendix. I can see you never heard of me before. You're still standing there. I am a man of infinite mercy, and I'll just let you go on grinning, stupid as it looks, until the westbound Santa Fe pulls in, about ten minutes from now."

Stringer nodded and said, "That's mighty generous of you, Blue Streak. But I just got here, no offense, and I just don't feel like another train ride so soon."

Behind him the barkeep moaned, "Jesus H. Christ, son. You've just been informed you are discussing travel plans with the one and original Blue Streak Bendix!"

Stringer ignored him as he asked the more frightful apparition whether it was speaking for the town, the county, or in view of its sweaty outfit, Los Estados Unido de Mejico. When Bendix spat and said he was just running a nosy stranger out of town on his own, from a sense of civic duty, Stringer laughed and said, "Hell, I thought I might be in trouble."

Behind him the only other man in the place muttered, "Oh, shit!" and began to take down the mirror as he added, "Let me get out of here first, boys. This ain't my fight and I don't want to watch."

Neither Stringer nor the man out to rawhide him replied as their only possible witness crawfished out of sight. Stringer waited until he was sure they had the place to themselves alone before he said, still pleasantly, "If we put our heads together, now that nobody's taking notes, we can still make it look like peace with honor. In a world of mostly sheep, nobody really expects the wolves to more than growl at one another, and that poor old barkeep we scared so bad is sure to report we both growled good. I don't think anyone's likely to call us sissies if we call this dumb situation a standoff based on mutual respect. So why don't we do that, pard?"

Blue Streak growled, "I didn't come here to be your pard. I was told to run you out of town, or failing that, to blow your nosy face off. So which way do you want to leave town, aboard that old train or in a new pine box?"

Stringer didn't answer as they locked eyes. Neither liked what he was staring into. Blue Streak's slitted eyes were an uncertain shade of blue or gray. Stringer's were more clinical than threatening, and were most often described as amber or old gold, in keeping with the overall bronze shade of his features and close-cut hair. At the moment they were cooling from a friendly gold to a pair of cold brass cannon muzzles trained on a pirate ship.

Blue Streak Bendix shifted his weight, either nervously or with deadly intent, and then Stringer simply drew and fired in one motion, knowing exactly what he was doing.

The bully he'd caught flatfooted staggered backward, crashed into a table, and did a back flip over it to wind up supine in a far corner, wheezing and bitching, as Stringer's smoking six-gun remained trained at its latest victim.

Stringer kicked the table between them out of the way. The man he'd put in the corner stared up owl-eyed and gasped, "I give! I give! You didn't have to act so mean, for God's sake!"

Stringer hunkered down to disarm the wounded gun slick, sliding both .45's aside across the sawdust before he proceeded to reload his double-action .38, muttering, "Never tell a grown man or even a tough-looking woman, in advance, that you are even considering gun play. I just showed you why. So let's discuss where you're hit, and how bad."

Blue Streak didn't answer. Stringer felt the side of his throat, tore open the black shirt under the dark leather bolero, and was rising to his feet when the old barkeep came back via the front entrance with a younger gent wearing a brass star and a dozen or so townies wearing the detached expressions common sense called for at times like these.

Stringer told the town law, "He's still alive. The bullet I put in his chest just now must have missed his heart and spine. We'd both be much obliged if any number of you gents went for the doctor about now."

One of the townies nodded and lit out, with a couple of others tagging after for whatever reason. The town law said, "I'd be much obliged if you'd hand that .38 to me, grips first, stranger."

Stringer shook his head and reholstered his sidearm instead as he said, "I'm not a stranger. My handle is Stuart MacKail and I'm a field stringer for the *San Francisco Sun*. You doubtless know who the gent in yon corner is." He nodded at the old barkeep and added, "This friendlier gent must have told you when he got to you that Old Blue Streak was trying to pick a fight with me."

The barkeep said, "That's true, Nate. I must say I would have put my money on the loser, never having seen this young rascal in action. But Blue Streak was the one who issued the invite. This newspaper man wasn't acting like he was looking for trouble, save for having a sort of curious nature."

The town law stared soberly at Stringer and said, "Old Jimbo, here, tells us you was asking questions about that murderous old Commodore Perry Owens just before Blue Streak, yonder, clouded up to rain on you. I don't suppose you'd like to explain?"

Stringer asked, "Explain what, how such a slow-moving cuss got the name of Blue Streak, or why I'm looking for Sheriff Owens?"

The brass badge growled, "Don't sass me, son. You're already in enough trouble if Bendix dies, and Owens ain't no such thing as a sheriff no more. So what do you want with the mean old goat?"

Stringer said, "I was sent to interview him. About

the old west he knew, and mayhaps how come the new west has no use for his kind anymore."

The lawman they called Nate grimaced and said, "Anyone can tell you that. There was a time when Holbrook might have needed a born killer to calm things down. We got at least fifty total strangers buried unmarked in our potter's field. This very saloon got named so quaint the night a Texican named Crawford got into an unfriendly card game with a bunch of Mexicans, resulting in more than one bucket full of blood spattered all the way from yon corner to the planks out front. Crawford was only one of such surly gents old Owens had to tame when town taming was the way us peace officers kept the peace. But Holbrook is more civilized these days, or was until a few minutes ago. So we don't cotton to such wild ways no more, and I'm still waiting for you to hand me your gun."

Stringer shook his head and said, "Not hardly. If I'm under arrest, I'll come with you to see the judge. But I have noticed in my travels that it's a lot easier to whip up a lynch mob than it is to go up against even one man able to defend himself. So I reckon I'll just stay able to defend myself until we see how many friends and admirers that rascal in yon corner may have in these parts."

A million tense years passed by before the brass badge proved himself wiser than the bully of the town by saying, "Well, seeing he ain't really dead yet, I reckon we can leave you in your own custody if you'll give us your word, as a man, you won't leave town until this matter get's cleared up tidy and lawsome."

Before Stringer could answer, the men who'd run

for the doctor were back with the same. Stringer stepped out of the officious little gent's way as he told the lawman, "You have my word. I wasn't planning on leaving Holbrook soon, in any case. That was what the fuss was all about. I wouldn't have had to shoot the silly bastard if he hadn't been trying to run me out of town."

The brass badge seemed satisfied. So Stringer moved closer to the corner, where the sawbones was squatting beside Blue Streak Bendix, cussing a blue streak. When he ran out of dirty words the medical expert opined, "He's lucky to be living in Arizona already. For that's where they usually advise lung cases to move. His right lung's collapsed, probably for keeps. But if infection don't set in too bad, he'll likely live. I'd sure like some help in getting him to the clinic, for he's one big son of a bitch, and he won't be up to walking for some time."

Stringer offered to help. But the lawman called Nate said, "I'd say you've done enough for him already today. If I was you, I'd be scouting up a lawyer about now. A good one."

Stringer nodded but said, "The doc says he'll likely live."

Nate said, "You'd still best find a good lawyer. Doc could be wrong, and like I said, these parts is run more stuffy these days than it was when one man could gun another and just walk away."

The law offices of Stern & Addams were above a barber shop just down the street from the Bucket of Blood. When Stringer entered, he was mildly surprised to see that Stern, Addams, or whoever, looked more like a pretty ash blonde of say thirty than his picture of a small-town lawyer. She looked up at him from behind her desk, and he had to give her credit for a pretty good poker face as she sized up his faded denims and battered Stetson. Before she could throw him out, he produced his press pass and said, "I'm not here about water rights or a boundary dispute, ma'am. I just shot a man, and the *San Francisco Sun* is willing to pay legal expenses as long as I can convince *them* I'm innocent."

She said, "Lawyer Addams has left for the day and may not be back for some time. He's out on the range, dealing with one of those water disputes you seem to find so silly. Nobody in this part of Arizona Territory takes water that lightly, Mr. MacKail. You might try Simon and Weddington, across from the courthouse."

Stringer shook his head and said, "I don't think I want any members of the current courthouse gang, ma'am. I took the liberty of asking about this firm, too, before I came to you with my troubles. They told me Lawyer Addams was a member of the party committee who backed Commodore Perry Owens in the last election."

"We lost." She sighed wearily.

He said, "I know. That's something else we have to talk about, after you get me off. If Lawyer Addams is gone for the day, how do I go about talking to his partner, Lawyer Stern?"

She sighed again and said, "You can't. I'm his widow, Patricia Stern. Everyone calls me Patty. I was left my husband's interest in the firm. But I just work here. The Arizona Bar Association is a bit old-fashioned about she-male lawyers, as they refer to the poor inferior beings."

Stringer said, "I hired a she-male lawyer once. She got me off as good as anyone else could have."

The attractive young widow tried not to smile as she pointed at the bentwood chair near one corner of her desk and said, "You may as well let me take some notes. But you understand I don't have any professional standing if they arrest you before the boss gets back, right?"

He swung the chair in place and straddled it, facing her. She listened quietly as he brought her up to date on his misadventure in the Bucket of Blood. He expected her to write down the name of the man he'd had to gun. But she didn't. She stared at him the way she might have stared at an unexpected notice from the tax collector as she marveled, "*You* got into a gun fight with Blue Streak Bendix, and won?"

He shrugged modestly and said, "I know I'm not as famous in these parts. That may have given me the edge I needed. Old Blue Streak has likely grown so accustomed to crawfishing everyone he blusters to that he's forgotten how to streak."

She said, "Well, you'll surely be better known around here now. You say he picked on you for no reason at all, ah . . . Stuart?"

He winced and said, "Call me Stringer, Patty. I don't know why my folks named me after a string of losers, but they were Scotch and tended to excuse the royal clan for it's self-destructive stubborn streak. I didn't say Bendix started up with me for no reason at all. He made it plain he wanted me to leave Holbrook on the next train out. He also slipped up enough to mention some *they* who'd told him to run me or gun me. I'd like to talk to him about that some more, as soon as he's up to receiving visitors. So what I need from you is a writ or whatever allowing me to sort of wander about unmolested until he dies or gets better."

She was working at her shorthand now as she told him, "The county coroner has no call to bother you as long as the man you shot is still alive. The town marshal could probably run you in for disturbing the peace. But since he hasn't, he's probably as interested as we are about the outcome of the poor brute's chest wound. He himself has the right to prefer charges against you when he feels up to it."

Stringer asked, "Can't I press charges against him, for starting the fight in the first place?"

She said, "That's what I'm writing. It will look longer and a lot stuffier after I type it up in legal jargon. But in essence what we want to charge him with is attempted murder after you refused his unseemly advances, right?"

Stringer frowned and said, "Hold on. I never said Blue Streak struck me as one of them swishy gents. That's an awful thing to accuse another man of, and fair is fair. He didn't act near that friendly in the Bucket of Blood, Patty."

She asked, "Who's writing this complaint up, you or me? Every little bit helps, and who's to say whether he dressed so fancy to impress boys or girls, if he dies?"

Stringer shook his head and said, "I can see you're out to get the jump on his lawyer by casting the first horse apple, Patty. But I won't sign such a whopper about a fellow man. He wasn't out to kiss me. He was out to kill me. Or he said he was. I had no intention of waiting for him to prove he meant it, which is why he shouldn't have said it if he didn't. I hardly ever gun a man who doesn't have a gunning coming. So whether he lives or not, I stand ready to defend my action in court fair and square with the simple truth."

She shrugged and crossed a line out, saying, "It's a good thing this is Arizona Territory instead of Holland. You must be awfully dangerous to let loose near windmills. But very well, the man does enjoy a certain rep as a bully, and it is unconstitutional to run innocent people out of town without a peace writ or even a badge. Where will you be staying while you're here in Holbrook, ah . . . Stringer?"

He shrugged and said, "I don't know. I figured I needed a lawyer more than I needed a place to bunk. So I came here first. Do you know a good hotel in town?"

She grimaced and said, "*Good* would hardly be the word for the Majestic. But they say none of the bugs are big as the rats, at least. It's just across from the water tower near the tracks. Don't say I sent you. The unspeakable woman who runs the place hates me too."

He chuckled and said, "Holbrook sure is a friendly little old town. I'll study the vermin at the Majestic later. First I got to look up old Commodore Perry Owens."

She asked, "Oh, do you know the poor old dear?"

He replied, "Not yet. Do you?"

She nodded and said, "Ever since I was a schoolgirl. We might not have had a school if it hadn't been for that gruff old huggy bear."

Stringer said, "I hear how Owens cleaned up the

whole county. Is that why you worked for his last election try?"

She nodded. "We all did. All of us old-timers who knew him, that is. It wasn't fair for the Republicans to run a younger, perhaps more educated man against Sheriff Owens, for before he made them stop, the cowhands around here used to shoot Republicans on sight. Most of the riders for the Aztec Land and Cattle Company came west with the railroad from Texas, you see."

He said, "I heard the Hash Knife brand was big and ferocious, and that Arizona country folk vote as solid a Democrat ticket as Texas always has. But I'd rather discuss the freak election with the man who lost it, no offense. So where can I find your old huggy bear these days?"

She sighed and said, "I don't know. He took it awfully hard. They say that the morning after the final votes had been tallied, he stood tall in front of the courthouse, threw his tin star down in the street, and ground it into the dust with his boot heel. Then he got in his buckboard with his pretty young wife, Miss Elizabeth, and drove away, not looking back. They never went back to their spread here in Navajo County. Some say he was so bitter he just kept driving, forever."

A hearty male voice behind Stringer asked, "Who drove where forever, Patty?" and Stringer turned to see a tall portly man of about fifty. He looked like a born politician to Stringer. But his smile seemed sincere and his handshake was as firm as they were introduced. Lawyer Addams made them follow him into his somewhat more imposing oak-paneled private office and tell him the whole story again. Stringer was getting mighty sick of it by the time they had Addams up to date, with Patty doing most of the talking. Her boss or senior partner, whichever, nodded thoughtfully at Stringer and said, "I'm sure I can get one of the few honest judges we have left to set you free without bail, on paper I mean. I'll ask him for a peace bond and a formal permit for that gun of yours while I'm at it. Meanwhile, you'd best hole up at the Majestic until we can arm you properly for this infernal Republican town."

Stringer asked thoughtfully, "How come I have to hide out at all? Nobody's tried to arrest me so far."

Lawyer Addams smiled knowingly and asked, "Who could blame our new town marshal, Nate Ryan, after you'd just beaten the former quick-draw champ of the county to the draw? But Nate's just a chore boy to the powers that be, and we've agreed Blue Streak was sent to run you out of town by someone more important. The next gun slick who tries is likely to come at you with a badge as well as more backing. Let us back you with your own legal standing in this community, and the odds will be more even. Right now you're just a stranger who sassed the town law after gunning a local citizen. Do you really need a diagram on the blackboard to see how they could make that read for the coroner's jury later?"

Stringer smiled thinly and said, "I figured I'd be smarter coming to a lawyer who's no longer in with the courthouse gang. What kind of a retainer did you have in mind?"

Lawyer Addams shrugged and said, "I know

where you work, should you skip out on your final fee. I frankly can't say, this early, how much money we'll be talking about by the time this is over. So far we haven't done more than twenty dollars worth of anything for you. It's only fair to warn you that we could be talking three or even four figures by the time you're free to leave town, though."

Stringer grimaced and said, "Had I known old Sheriff Owens had already done so, I might have taken that fool's advice about the next train out. I don't see how I'll ever dig up enough of a story to even pay for the trip, with the star attraction pouting somewhere off stage."

Addams nodded understandingly and said, "I may be able to give you a few names, dates, and places later, when we've more time to chat. Owens and me go back a ways. I even rode with him on posse a time or two, when the world and us were younger and wilder. But right now you'd best get over to that hotel and stay out of sight until I can get to a judge who recalls the old days as fondly."

Stringer agreed. But as he was leaving he turned in the doorway to say, "Miss Patty, here, told me Owens and his wife drove off forever, leaving their property here to whom? It seems to me that even a bitter man would want *something* for his property."

Addams nodded and said, "He did. I handled the sale for them. Before you ask, no, I don't have their present address. I wired the money to a hotel in Globe. The next time I tried to get in touch with my old pal, they'd checked out of the hotel and left no forwarding address. They might be ranching down that way, or even farming some of that new irrigated cropland along the Gila. I know he hasn't pinned on another badge. Not in this territory, at any rate. I asked."

Stringer asked, "How come? Was it that important?"

Addams said, "Not really, but I try to do right by my clients or former clients. Mrs. Owens, the former Elizabeth Barrett, had credit coming to her at the dry goods store. Old Pear, that's what his pals were allowed to call him, had given them a couple of hundred dollars for his wife to charge against. She hadn't charged near that much when they left town so suddenly. So, as they knew I handled some business for them, the store owners gave me the unspent money to give back to them. I tried. But as I said, they'd just dropped out of sight. I imagine Pear thought his wife had spent most of it on female notions, and she—being a woman—didn't understand she had anything coming back to her." Then he noticed the dirty look he was getting from Patty Stern and quickly added, "It was Patty, here, who came up with the grand suggestion we bank the money for them in escrow so's it can be earning interest while we figure out where in thunder they might be these days."

All three of them grinned knowingly. Then the blonde walked Stringer to the hallway, told him she'd get his papers to him by sundown at the latest, and warned him, "Take Lawyer Addams serious, no matter how fat and jolly he looks. He's practiced law here in Navajo County since they were calling it part of Apache County, and it's true he's ridden all over it on posse as well as business. So he knows the way things work in this rustic corner of the territory, and if he says you ought to watch yourself, you'd just better watch yourself, hear?"

He said he'd already figured Addams for a sly as well as tail-wagging old dog, and they parted friendly.

CHAPTER
THREE

It was now mid-afternoon, but not as hot, for the sun had been ambushed by some unseasonable summer clouds—thunderheads, from the way they growled as well as looked. He was glad he had the rain slicker in his gladstone as he trudged toward the railroad tracks with it in his left hand. He spotted the water tower before he spotted anything that looked like a Majestic Hotel, and when he did see the once-gilt letters across the false front, he had to laugh. For while the frame structure was two stories high, sort of, it was too rinky-dink to qualify as noble, and to hell with Her Majesty.

Once inside, though, he was pleasantly surprised by the smell of the small dark lobby. Someone had used a lot of lemon oil on the woodwork, and there was a big cut-glass bowl of fresh-cut red roses on the check-in counter, stinking pretty as anything.

The severely handsome woman behind the counter didn't seem to admire him half as much, though. He figured her for about forty, depending on how life had treated her. Her dark brown hair was bunned up so tight atop her skull he figured it had to be smoothing at least a few wrinkles from her priss-lipped face. She'd have still been sort of pretty if the hotel business hadn't no doubt given her just cause to regard guests dressed as cowboys with considerable dismay.

He said, "I know I'm not wearing a proper tie, and I agree this gladstone don't look loaded with treasure, ma'am. So before you tell me all your rooms are chock full of less uncouth gents, I'd best show you my credentials and lay some money on you in advance."

Her expression didn't change until she'd had time to admire his press pass and a portrait Andrew Jackson. Then her face got almost human as she asked, "How long will you be staying with us, Mr. Mac-Kail? I notice you spell that M-A-C, rather than M-C."

He said, "I'm not sure how long I'll have to stay here in Holbrook, ma'am. You just tell me when I've used up that twenty and I'll give you some more. My name's always been spelled that way because that's the way it was spelled in the old country, which was Lochaber, County Inverness."

She actually managed a frosty smile as she took down his key and said, "I'll show you to your room, then. My name is MacLean, Margaret MacLean, County Argyll, by the way."

That didn't surprise Stringer. Nobody else ever seemed to worry about whether it was Mac or Mc. She was a long way from a wee lassie as he followed her up the narrow stairs to the top floor. But she sure hour-glassed nicely under that starched white blouse and chocolate brown skirt that buttoned down the side in the new and somewhat shocking fashion, even if you couldn't see anything.

She led him into a small but clean room with a mighty slanting ceiling. He'd noticed out front that the building was only built square in front. He'd given up trying to figure out false fronts. They never fooled anyone, and had to be more expensive than honest carpentry. He put down his gladstone and said the quarters suited him just fine.

She said, "Well, I'd best get downstairs and wait for the 2:47. I know nobody ever gets off that train, but you never know."

He nodded and said he could see a lady in the hotel business would have to be up on her railroad timetables. She smiled sort of wistfully and said, "That's not where I learned about railroad matters. I used to be a Harvey Girl. But what am I saying? You can't be old enough to remember the Harvey Girls."

He suspected she was hoping that wasn't true. So he said, "Sure I remember the Harvey Girls along the Santa Fe, Miss Margaret. They served coffee and grub all along the right of way until the Pullman dining cars got invented." Then, as he counted in his head and saw how the years added up, he gallantly added, "I hope you won't get sore. But if you was ever a Harvey Girl, you sure must have signed on for the last season, younger than they should have hired you. For you look more like a Gibson Girl than any Harvey Girl."

She looked flustered and told him he was just an old fibber, adding, "My friends call me Madge. I kill when I hear Maggie. I have to go now. Make yourself at home, and don't you go flattering my wallpaper, even if you are a Lochaber man!"

He didn't see fit to argue that he considered himself a Mother Lode rider, to the extent he worried about such notions. When she left, he proceeded to get comfortable, and found himself wondering why some folk worried so about their old countries. Perhaps, having grown up on a spread where all the neighbors had been either Scotch or Mexican, and knowing he was Americano, he'd just naturally assumed that all Americans were his kind of folk. He hadn't really noticed, until he'd gone off to Cuba with the Rough Riders as a young and green war correspondent, how many odd kinds of white folk and even colored folk called themselves Americans.

When he got down to his socks, jeans, and undershirt, Stringer sat on the narrow but comfortable brass-bound bed to roll a smoke and try to get back to serious matters. He didn't care what kind of a name Owens was, even if it did sound Welsh. He hadn't come all this way to study the old sheriff's family tree. The story, if there was a story, lay in how he'd been crooked out of office—and just as important, why?

It was a pure fact of nature that most cowtowns tended to be run by Republicans, as merchants and bankers tended to be, and that just the same, most such communities were content with a Democrat county sheriff to police the surrounding countryside, which was almost always solid Democrat country, here in the southwest. Both parties knew that made good sense. The notorious gun fight at the OK Corral, which had really taken place in a vacant lot across the street, until editors like Sam Barca had thought that less interesting, never would have happened had the voters of Tombstone not elected two separate and surly cliques of rival parties to police the infernal town at the same time.

That confusion had been settled back about the time this fool town was being born. They'd had the sense to put in a sheriff who spoke the same politics as the cowhands he stopped from shooting up the business establishments owned mostly by Damn-Yankee Republicans, Mormons, and other natural targets of the Texican yahoo. Owens had done a good job for a long time. So something about Navajo County had changed, a lot, if even the local Democrats had voted him out.

Stringer started to light his Bull Durham. A big fat crystal globe crashed down from the sky to the hitherto dry sill of the one open window and spattered all over him, snuffing his match.

He said, "Aw, hell," and rose to close the window as it began to rain fire and salt outside. He was facing the water tower across the way as he did so. So he saw the dark figure atop it, training a rifle his way, and ducked just in time.

As Stringer hit the rug a big buffalo round—from the sound of it—smashed through one pane to shower him with powdered glass and let the rain come in even more. Stringer cursed, rolled to the chair he'd draped his gun rig over, and crawled back to the window to return the compliment.

He reached up to slide the window open again, braced for a mighty hard slap on the wrist. When nothing like that happened, he risked his head above the sill as far as his cheekbones, as one had to in order to find a target at times like these. But he saw no target now. It was even hard to make out the water tower, with the desert cloudburst waving silvery veils of downpour back and forth. When he did get a clear view, during a shift of the wind, he saw nobody up there.

The door opened behind him. Stringer almost shot poor old Madge before he saw who'd circled behind him. He snapped, "Get down, damn it!" and when, instead, she came closer, demanding to know what on earth he was doing to her very own property, he kicked her ankles out from under her with a fortunately bootless foot.

She sure yelled a lot, for a gal who couldn't be that hurt, as she landed almost on top of him. Her head was still above the level of the windowsill. He grabbed her hair bun with his free hand and shoved her face to the floor as she proceeded to beat her rug with her fists and yell rape, murder, or both.

He shook her to shut her up and hissed, "I ain't out to rape you, no offense. We're under fire from that tower across the way. Or we was, until just recent. Lay still while I figure out who may or may not be shooting at us."

She propped herself up on one elbow, staring about in wonder at the glass and raindrops on her rug as she moaned, "Oh, Lord, my grandmother often warned us about Lochaber men. You haven't been under my roof a full hour and you've wrecked the place!"

He smiled reassuringly at her. It was easier to smile at her now that her soft brown hair was hanging down like that and she'd somehow lost the two top buttons of her blouse. He said, "I never done it. But I'll clean it up and even pay for a new pane. Our more important chore at the moment is to stay alive long enough to worry about housekeeping chores. Did anyone come in off that last train?"

She said, "No. We're all alone here. There are no other guests. But surely help is on the way by now, if you heard gun shots."

He said, "I heard one. Did you?"

She gave a little moan and answered, "No. Not that I noticed above that storm outside and— Oh, Stuart, what will we ever do to save ourselves?"

He said, "Nothing. We don't have to do anything, whether he's gone or taking one hell of a shower bath right now. He missed his one good chance as I was sitting near an open window like a fool. I'm a lot harder to hit once I know someone's shooting at me. He likely knows that, too, by now. His best chance to get away will be during this gully washer, with nobody else out of doors."

She asked, "What if they decide that makes this a good time to move in on us . . . and who on earth are they?"

He said, "If I knew the answer to either of your questions, I'd know what's going on. They're not after *us*. I told you they were shooting at *me*. They wouldn't have even known which window to shoot at if I hadn't been too addled by the heat to think straight after I'd been *told* someone wanted me out of town or dead."

She glanced up through the wet glass and said, "Well, it's going to cool off a lot before we see the sun again. The wind is from the east, and in these parts that means the thunderbird is serious. By the time this storm lets up it may be too late for anyone decent to be out and about. The streets of Holbrook are mighty quiet after dark when the herd's not in town."

As if to show how noisy the streets of Holbrook could get, a thunderbolt sizzled down, close enough to shake the whole hotel, and she clutched at him to bury her face against his undershirt, gasping, "Oh, Stuart, I'm so scared! *Do* something!"

He patted her back to comfort her, saying, "Steady, now. I don't think anyone yellow enough to snipe from such uncertain range is likely to move in on an armed enemy, on the alert and forted up. But it might be a good notion to be fort up better. They have this room figured. Are the doors downstairs locked?"

She said, "My back door's bolted good. I don't cotton to tramps stealing grub from my kitchen pantry while I'm minding the front. The door you came in by is shut, I hope, but of course it's not locked. I have enough trouble getting anyone to stay here as it is."

He said, "Bueno. Here's what we'll do. First we check out of this room and into one that covers the stairwell better. Then I'll go down and bar the front door. Coming in, front or back, they'll have to make some noise, and should they be dumb enough to come at us up that narrow stairway, it'll be my turn to make some noise, see?"

She did. She started to rise. He hauled her back down and said, "Crawling only takes a little longer, and it can be a lot better for your health. You go first and let me cover your rear."

She did, laughing like hell, as if he'd said something funny.

As her well padded but shapely rump swung out

of sight around the doorjamb, Stringer gathered the things he'd shucked out of and followed. It seemed safe to stand up in the hallway. So he did. He saw she was still on her hands and knees as she moved into the other room at the head of the stairs. He tossed his things in after her and moved down the stairs in his stocking feet, gun in hand. It only took him a few seconds to bar the heavy front door on the inside. Some of its weight was thick glass. It looked harder to bust than the front window beside the door. Either way, anyone that serious about busting in would have to make considerable noise.

Having done what he could down below, Stringer glanced out through the door glass to see the street out front was doing it's damnedest to look like a river. The muddy water was ankle deep and trying to figure some place to go as the heavy rain kept frothing it deeper. He smiled crookedly, said, "Drown, you sons of bitches!" and went back upstairs to see how old Madge was making out.

He stopped in the doorway to stare down at the somewhat bigger bedstead in the somewhat bigger room, somewhat confused. For his landlady lay under the sheets, her hair now completely unbound and draped becomingly down on her bare shoulders, while her Gibson Girl blouse and skirt lay on the rug near his own carelessly tossed duds, as if she'd shucked in a hurry. He saw no underwear. She was likely still wearing it.

He said, "Well, this is sure an odd time to be taking a siesta."

She smiled invitingly up at him and said, "Get under these covers with me. It's gotten so cool and clammy everywhere else that you're just asking for a chill in that undershirt, you poor boy."

He considered his shirt and jacket on the floor between them. Then he wondered why anyone would want to consider a stupid move like that. He chuckled and said, "I admire your sense of timing. Has it occured to you we're supposed to be under siege right now?"

She said, "Pooh, there's room for your six-gun as well as the two of us in this bed, and in any case, they'd have come by now if they really meant to come, right?"

He said he guessed so, and left the door ajar as he moved over to join her. He still had his jeans, socks, and undershirt on as he slid under the covers with her. He found her waiting clad in nothing but her high-button shoes and black silk stockings. Not sure just how else one might get in bed with a naked lady, he put his six-gun on the bed table and took her in his arms. He could tell it was the proper move with such an unusual landlady when she swarmed all over him at once, kissing and scratching as she tore at his pants to get them out of the way. He helped her. Most men would have by this time, even if he was still surprised if not as confused about her notions of forting up against the rest of the world. Then they let the rest of the world worry about its own damn self for a long sweet time as the raindrops drummed on the slanting roof above the bed and the bed made considerable noise of its own beneath their tightly entwined and grinding flesh.

When they finally had to stop to catch their second winds, she moaned, "Oh, that was heavensome, darling. But don't take it out. Please don't take it out. It's been so long since I've had anything that deep in my poor old worn-out frame."

He didn't doubt a gal would have to be sort of hard up to make the first move so direct. He knew she wanted him to call her a liar about her poor old worn-out frame, so he moved in it teasingly as he said, "Come on, Madge. You're built like a teenager and you know it." Which, in fact, was the simple truth. For though her face still looked a mite old for him, even after all that kissing, time's cruel teeth hadn't gotten at her firm and satin-smooth body enough to notice yet.

She wrapped her long, still shapely legs around his waist, locking her high-button kid shoes atop his naked tailbone, and hugged him tighter everywhere as she moaned, "Oh, Jesus, when I think of the teenage years I wasted, I could cry. I came out here to work for Harvey as a virgin, Stuart. I was almost twenty-five when a no-good tin-horn gambler I'll always remember with gratitude done me wrong."

He started moving in response to her contractions as he told her, "I feel sort of grateful to him, too, right now. He sure broke you in mighty fine."

She said, "Don't talk dirty. I wasn't sure I liked it this much the first time, and I cried fit to bust when that mean old sheriff ran him out of town."

Stringer didn't know why gals liked to confess more than any man might want to hear at times like these, and like most men, he found such conversation more distasteful than romantic. Then she said, "Once I felt less shy about romance, I started to get really good at it."

He didn't answer. For she was good at it indeed, and though he knew he shouldn't be enjoying himself this much in such rough company, he felt it all the way down to his socks when they came together again.

But as sanity returned, as it ever must, Stringer rolled off and said, "Somebody ought to check that front door again, and I can see you're not as interested."

She told him he had a lovely body as he rose and moved out of the room and down the stairs to where he could see the front door. It was as securely barred as ever, and the flood water out front was now lapping at the plank walks. He rejoined Madge to say, "If this rain keeps up, they'll have to come at us in a canoe. I hope you don't have a cellar to worry about."

She said she didn't, and added, "This used to be the Harvey House when the world and me was younger. I had it hauled over from the tracks in one piece, after Harvey went out of business."

Then she started to cry.

Stringer put the .38 back on the table and climbed in to comfort her, asking her what was wrong as he held her now trembling body close, in a more brotherly way than before.

She sobbed, "Oh, Stuart, time flows so swiftly by, and we get so little of it as our share. It seems like yesterday I came out here as a wide-eyed innocent, and I still don't feel like the legend of the past I guess I really am."

He kissed her gently and lowered them both to the pillows again as he said, "Hell, you're not as ancient as the Butterfield Stage the Santa Fe put out of business. Time changes faster than it really passes, Madge. I deal in legends, more than I want to, thanks to a boss who can't get enough of what he calls the old west. Looking back, things that lasted not much longer than a mayfly seem like historic eras. But they weren't. They were just emergency measures. To hear old-timers tell it, everyone who ever rode a horse west of the Mississippi rode for the pony express in the few short months it was in business. Now that the Harvey Girl era has been over a spell, folk think of you old-timers as a sort of permanent fixture of a past that never was. But we both know that short-lived restaurant chain was little more than a quick-buck slicker's clever notion that was too good to last."

She sighed and said, "It was grand, while it lasted. It was mean of the railroad to start running dining cars just as we was getting to be famous and admired. Mr. Harvey was a decent boss who paid us fair wages and looked after us as if we was his own. He'd fire a girl if she got in trouble, or even fat. He told us we had standards to meet, and we met 'em. We kept ourselves neat and slung good hash. Ask any old-timer and they'll tell you the food on the dining cars has never been as good as the food we served, cheaper."

He said, "I told you we live in changing times. Let's talk of more important matters an old-timer in these parts might know more than me about. You said your first boyfriend was run off by the sheriff. Would that have been Sheriff Commodore Perry Owens?"

She sniffed and said, "Of course. We never had no other sheriff, until recent. I was mad as anything when he ran off my gambling man. But fair is fair, and I have to say old Pear kept the lid on things in these parts, once he got a lid on it, I mean. Holbrook was a mighty wild little town when I first saw it. Pear got the job because nobody else was tough enough to want it. Nobody expected him to live twenty-four hours, let alone the almost twenty years he lasted. You see, he was a sort of sissy-looking gent in his younger days. He wore his hair longer than General Custer, even after Custer cut his own more fashionable and got killed for his trouble. They say Pear had been an Indian fighter, too, before he took up the law as his career. He dressed cow, but sort of fancy, with a hat brim big enough to run a toy train on, and silver conchos stuck all over him. But nobody laughed at him as much after he stopped a showdown between some Texas hands and a bunch of Mex vaqueros by standing in the middle, alone, and telling one and all he'd gun the first son of a bitch who went for his guns. He talked that rough to everyone. When anyone said *he* was a son of a bitch, Pear pistol-whipped impartial, be it Tex, Mex, Mormon, or Gentile, until everyone admired him for his fairness. They say he was the first county official who ever kept proper books, too. Old Judge Wattron, who was either a J.P., the town marshal, or a druggist, depending on the time of day, stole everything that wasn't nailed down before they voted him out."

Stringer asked, "Was Owens accused of such dishonest habits before or during the last election?"

She shrugged her bare shoulder against him and said, "No. Even the Republicans allowed old Pear was upright and true. They just said it was time for a change, and I reckon a lot of folk must've thought so too. I'd have voted for Pear, if women were allowed to vote. Women liked him. Not this way—he never messed with any of us. But we could see he was a gent of the old school, and he made it safe for us to go shopping, even when the herd was in town. Nobody ever got fresh with gals while old Pear was running things in this county."

Stringer remembered another lady who didn't seem to admire old Madge had told him much the same thing. He muttered, "Sam Barca could be on to something. A popular lawman gets rooked out of office, and when outsiders ask how come, they get shot at."

She began to fondle him teasingly as she said, "I think the rain's letting up. We'd better get this sweet thing up again before this hotel has to get back in business."

He thought that was a grand notion. But just as she'd kissed her way down his bare belly far enough to really matter, they both heard someone pounding on the door downstairs. Madge said, "Damn. We'll have to start from scratch, later tonight. For I know that knock of old."

She tossed the covers aside and rolled over him, inspiringly, to start dressing with astounding speed. As Stringer sat up with gun in hand, she said, "It's not them. It's him. Nate Ryan, the town marshal. Nobody else knocks so bossy. I'd best go down and see what he wants."

As she left, pinning her hair back up on the fly, Stringer swung his socks to the rug and began to haul his own duds on just in case. He was glad he had when, a few moments later, Madge reappeared in the doorway with the brass-badged Ryan. The town law said, "I'll take the .38, now, and this time I really

STRINGER ON DEAD MAN'S RANGE

mean it, MacKail. I'm here to arrest you for the murder of Blue Streak Bendix."

Stringer frowned and said, "I'm sorry he died. But murder is putting it a mite strong, Nate. I put that bullet in him in self-defense."

Ryan said, "Not the one in his head that killed him. The doc said Bendix was sedated unconscious, flat on his back in bed, when you crept into the clinic and blew his brains out!"

Stringer whistled tunelessly and said, "I'm sorry about that too! I wanted to interview him some as soon as he was fit to give interviews. When did all this happen?"

The lawman said, "During the storm that just passed over, of course. Nobody downstairs heard the shot. What did you do, wait for a handy thunder clap?"

Stringer shook his head and said, "It wasn't me. I was here at this hotel from the first raindrop to the last."

"Can you prove it?" asked the lawman.

Stringer glanced at Madge, who was now managing to look as starchy as ever. She said, "He's telling it true, Nate. I stand ready to swear under oath I never saw him leave the premises since he checked in, well before the storm."

It wasn't good enough. Nate Ryan shrugged and said, "With all that wind and thunderation, he could have snuck out and back in easy enough. The clinic's just down the street, an easy dash for any man, and the doc says Blue Streak was shot twice, with a .38. So with all due respect to a lady's hearing during a thunderstorm—"

"Oh, for heavens sake, we were in bed together at

the time of the killing," she cut in, red-faced but head held high.

The town law's jaw dropped. He stared past her at the rumpled bed. Then he gulped and asked, "Would you be willing to swear to that under oath, ma'am?"

She sniffed and said, "If I have to. I don't want to, but I'd rather be shamed than see an innocent man hanged."

The brass badge looked uncertainly at Stringer and asked what he had to say about all this. Stringer said, "Nothing. Pay no mind to her. I'd confess to a crime I didn't commit before I'd let a lady dishonor herself on my account."

Nate Ryan let them wait a long tense time before he nodded and said, "I reckon I would too. So suffice it to say I see no need to doubt the word of another gent. If you was here at the time Blue Streak was murdered, I can't hardly arrest you for it, can I?"

Stringer gravely held out his hand and they shook on it. Then Nate said, "Aw, mush. Now I got to go scout up any sign the real killer might have left."

Stringer said, "Try around the water tower across the way," and when Nate asked him why, he explained, "Someone pegged a shot at me from there, just as the storm started. He might or might not have left signs that all that rain couldn't wash away. I don't suspect he was shooting at me just because he took me for a fat old quail. Someone didn't want me asking Blue Streak any questions. It seems likely that failing to get me, they had to shut Blue Streak up as best they knew how."

Nate said, "That makes sense, to a point. But the dormer window in this room don't face no water tower and— Never mind. I'd best go have a look anyway."

As he turned to clomp downstairs alone, Madge turned to her younger guest to sob, "Did you really mean that, about me being a lady?"

He nodded soberly and said, "I did. I'll allow I might have just thought you was a Harvey Girl, until you proved what a lady you really are, Miss Margaret MacLean."

CHAPTER
FOUR

Another lady, called Stern, showed up at the hotel just at sundown. Since she'd said she might, Stringer was waiting for her in the lobby, and when he spotted her through the front window, he stepped out to meet her. She'd told him how she felt about old Madge, and while he didn't share her loathing, he could sort of see why she might feel that way.

The younger woman greeted him with mud on her skirts and a smile on her lips before she told him, "I have enough court stays to keep Butch Cassidy out of jail, if they were made out in his name. But now we have to go to the hearing. You heard the news about that man you shot?"

He nodded, took the writs she handed him, stuffed them in a hip pocket, and took her arm as he swung out to the muddy side, asking, "Where is the coroner's jury meeting, and how come so late, Patty?"

She said, "I suppose they want to get it over during the cool of evening, thanks to that heaven-sent rain we were blessed with this afternoon. Wasn't that something?"

He said, "I sure enjoyed the surprise. Are we headed right?"

She said, "Yes, they're meeting over the drugstore next to the Bucket of Blood."

They were indeed. They'd already started by the time Patty Stern led him in by one hand. The county coroner was the same old doc who'd given first-aid to Bendix in the saloon next door. Stringer felt somehow sure that whatever the cause of death they might decide on, improper medical attention would hardly be it. He saw Lawyer Addams seated with the other mostly middle-aged and town-dressed gents behind the trestle table. As if he'd read Stringer's mind, Addams nodded their way, rose to his feet, and said, "I'm not sure I should take formal part in these proceedings, Doc. Young MacKail, here, is a client of mine."

The coroner growled, "Oh, sit down and behave yourself, W.R. We all know you're an ethical cuss, for a lawyer leastways, and Nate Ryan's already cleared this young gent."

He pointed at Stringer and said, "You sit down, too, young gent. We know you didn't shoot Bendix, that second time. But you may be able to shed some light on how come he was so popular."

Stringer drew up a folding chair, sat down, and told them all he knew, which might have been more than some of them really wanted to know, judging from the way a couple of the older panel members were yawning by the time he'd finished.

The old doc was made of sterner stuff. He thanked Stringer for his testimony and said, "Well, as I see it.

This newspaper man could be on to something. It seems obvious Blue Streak was sent to run him or gun him, by someone who didn't want something printed in any newspaper. We can assume it wasn't an original notion on Blue Streak's part, because he was never knowed as a heavy thinker, and even if he had been, he didn't commit suicide this afternoon. He was gunned severe by someone who took said gun with him on the way out. Anyone can see the killer had to be working for the same son of a bitch who hired Blue Streak to begin with. So all we have to figure out now is who said son of a bitch might be. Wake up, Sam. I'm open to sensible suggestions, from anyone here more sober."

Stringer waited, saw nobody else seemed willing to start, and said, "I was sent here to do a feature on Sheriff Owens and the election he lost a short spell back. I had announced such an intent shortly before Blue Streak showed up to inform me I was just too nosy for this town. He looked like no more than a hired bravo to me too. So it seems obvious someone more important has a guilty secret worth killing to hide."

The doc sighed and said, "Hell, anyone can see that, young man. What we don't know is the secret the bastard finds so all-fired important. It can't be anything Pear Owens could have told you if he was still in these parts. He left here mad as a wet hen and had he had any charge to make, he'd have surely made it, loud and clear. For he accused his political enemies of every damn thing he could come up with, some of it sort of silly."

Lawyer Addams said, "Aside from that, the one or more who sent Blue Streak after my client, here, had to know there was no way old Pear could betray said secret, even if he knew it."

An old gent who'd been leaning back with his eyes shut sat up straighter. "That's right," he said. "They couldn't have been trying to stop this young gent from talking to Owens. Everyone knows Owens and his wife ain't here in Navajo County no more."

The doc growled, "I just said that, damn it. So what's left?"

Stringer said, "I was sent here to cover your last election as well, and no offense, my editor thinks it could have been unfair."

There was a mutual murmur of outraged innocence. The coroner turned to Lawyer Addams and said, "You tell him, you durned old Democrat."

Addams smiled sadly and said, "I'm afraid my old pal Pear was a sore loser, MacKail. He cussed me good too. But as a member of the bipartisan committee overseeing the election results, I had to tell him we got licked fair and square. We did recount the ballots from some outlying districts we'd always been able to count on in the past. We did look into the charges Pear made about the other side counting the votes of gents he'd shot, personal. But the few voters named Grant or Tewksbury who voted Republican were not close kin to those two clans he ran out years ago. He didn't want to face it. He swore he'd been cheated. But I have to admit the other side simply gathered more votes. It can happen, even in Arizona Territory."

The coroner nodded and said, "There you go, son. I was on the committee to make sure the Democrats didn't vote too many tombstones, and though it pains me to say it, they didn't. The election returns are a matter of public record. They were already printed in the papers. Some papers were surprised as old Pear was, and you wasn't the first reporter to come here demanding a recount. So that couldn't have been why someone sent Blue Streak to run you out of town, right?"

Stringer said, "I don't know. They moved in on me before I got to ask many questions. With all due respect, I can see how a long-incumbent and popular sheriff might have found the election returns dismaying. It's a simple fact of nature that Arizona did vote nearly solid Democrat in that election everywhere else, and that here in Navajo County most of the rural voters and at least a third of the urban voters are, to this date, still registered as Democrats. So, no offense, it don't add up to me, either, and I vote independent."

Lawyer Addams sighed and said, "I've already been over that, loud, with old Pear, son. What you both noticed is true. Had everyone voted a straight-party ticket, Pear would have won by a landslide, as he no doubt expected. That's why we were careful to recount the ballots from some solid Democrat districts when they voted the other way. I don't know why, any more than Pear did. But the voters just turned against him, Republican and Democrat alike."

Stringer asked, "How come? There was no hint of recent scandal or even exciting gun play in the notes my editor gave me."

The coroner said, "As a member of the opposing camp I stand ready to say Commodore Perry Owens was an honest, upright gent of the old school. I was surprised, too, albeit delighted, at the way we skunked the infernal Democrats at last."

Lawyer Addams said, "As a member of the losing side I think I have the answer. You were all too correct when you said we'd had no recent excitement here in Navajo County, MacKail. I fear the voters forgot who made it possible for things to get so dull of late. I fear they lost respect for a no-longer-young man who wore his hair too long and dressed somewhat antique in fringed buckskin and Mex spurs that made him sound like Santa Claus as he strode about. I fear they wanted to keep up with the times, now that we're at the dawn of a new century and Geronimo has learned to sip Coca-Cola through a straw behind a stout reservation fence. They forgot who it was who held off the Apache when Geronimo was raising hell out here, and—"

"They was Navajo," the coroner cut in, adding, "Geronimo was too sissy to raid us when we was young and pretty, W.R. The redskins Owen shot it out with was Navajo, not Apache."

Lawyer Addams shrugged and said, "Just the same, Pear kept them away from our stock and womenfolk. He kept the Mexican raiders at bay too. I was there when he shot it out with old Martin Blevins and his five fire-eating sons, too, and no man here can tell me Blevins wasn't tougher than any damned Geronimo!"

The coroner said, "Simmer down, W.R. I never called this hearing to prove your old pal was a sissy. Pear Owens is gone. The election that sent him packing was as fair as elections ever can be in this imperfect world. So let's stick to guilty secrets in the here and now."

Adams thought, shrugged, then said, "I'm stumped. Nobody I know of is missing any stock.

Nobody has died mysterious recent, save for the late Blue Streak Bendix. Do we have any important court cases pending, Judge?"

The sleepy-looking but common-sense old cuss seated farther along the table opened his eyes again to say, "Nope. A nester called Riggins swore out a complaint about a Mex sheepherder a few weeks back. I told the fool Mex to keep his fool sheep out of the Riggins corn patch and he said he'd try. Neither one has the kind of money it would take to hire a gun. All I got on the docket at the moment is a divorce case, sort of. A Mormon gal holds—and I tend to agree—that it just ain't right for her husband to sleep with more than one woman at a time in Arizona Territory, no matter what their temple in Utah says."

He shot a sharp look at Stringer to ask, "Did you come here to write things about the Latter Day Saints, son?"

Stringer said, "Not hardly. That gal who claims to be one of Brigham Young's wives has already milked that angle, for all it's worth, in the book she published about her dreadful experience. Another Mormon gal I know says it's pure bull. I wouldn't know and I don't care. Besides, I wasn't talking about Mormons when Blue Streak advised me to leave town. I was talking about Sheriff Owens, and I still think that made someone tense as hell."

The coroner said, "This is getting us nowhere. As coroner of Navajo County I find the late Blue Streak Bendix was murdered in bed by a person or persons unknown, and the hell with it. It's up to the law to figure out who done it. So unless I hear some objection, and I'd better not, this hearing is over."

There was a murmur of agreement and a scraping of chairs as everyone but one old gent, sound asleep, got up. Stringer did the same and turned to see where Patty might be. She wasn't anywhere. That accounted for the coarse lingo, at least.

Lawyer Addams came over to join him, smiling, as he said, "I didn't think you had anything to worry about. Your paper owes us fifty bucks. I'll trust you for it if you're anxious to be on your way, MacKail."

Stringer said, "I'm not. I'll wire my boss for your fee. It sounds fair. But I mean to stick around until I get some answers."

Addams looked mildly surprised, but said, "I don't blame you. I'd want to know why someone pegged a shot at me too. But where on earth do you mean to start, son? The gents you were just talking to are the most important gents around here, and as you just heard, they can't figure it either."

Stringer said, "So they said. I don't reckon I'd blab any guilty secrets while I was sitting on a coroner's jury either."

The portly lawyer gasped and said, "Good Lord, I hope you're not suggesting that someone in this very room could be behind all this recent trouble!"

Stringer said, "I don't know. Someone has to be. I suspect the mastermind was, and is, afraid I'll stumble over something. I don't know what. Maybe Sheriff Owens or some of his other pals can tell me."

Addams said, "I'll see if I can locate him, then. I can't say I tried everything when all I was worried about was his wife's credit at the dry goods store. But even if we can locate him, what could he possibly tell us? He was and still is an honest lawman.

He'd have never just left, pissed off or not, had he known anything crooked was going on around here!"

Stringer nodded and said, "He might not have known what he was looking at. Patrolling so much territory, he might have heard or seen things he never added up. I suspect the rascal behind all this otherwise stupid gun play heaved one hell of a sigh of relief when Owens and his lady drove off, too sore to even think straight about a county that had turned on them. Since I can't ask them, I'll ask you what Owens was working on when he suddenly found himself out of office and off any cases he was covering. Would you know of any?"

Addams said, "Let's go next door for some brain tonic while I ponder that. Right now I'll be damned if I can recall any important cases within a year or more of the election."

They went downstairs and into the Bucket of Blood, where, to no great surprise, they found half the old gents from upstairs enjoying a chance to stay out a mite late for married men on a weeknight.

As Stringer and Lawyer Addams bellied up to the bar, Addams said, "Nope. It was like I said. I fear poor Pear lost because he just hadn't been up to anything interesting for a good many years. Civilization caught up with an old-style sheriff even before old age could. Pear would only be about fity right now, wherever the hell he may be tonight."

An even older gent from upstairs, standing on the far side of Addams, chimed in with, "Fifty-one. I know because when he was courting that pretty Miss Lizzie a year ago, the womenfolk said it was a scandal for a fifty-year-old man to chase after a gal so young." He inhaled some more suds before he added, "Womenfolk are like that. When they got their own sights set on such a gent, he's distinguished. When another gal is getting a gent of substance and property, he's an old goat."

Stringer asked Addams, "What was the last important case your old pal worked on, no matter how far back?"

Addams frowned and said, "I can't think of one within the last ten years or more."

The windy older man volunteered, "I can. What about the killing of Tom Graham, down Pleasant Valley way?"

Addams snorted in disgust and said, "Oh, for God's sake, that was back in '92, and outside Pear's jurisdiction to begin with."

The older man said, "It was still mysterious as hell, and you know Pear never worried about jurisdiction. Didn't he stop the Hash Knife War that time, county lines be damned?"

Addams rolled his eyes heavenward and muttered, "Now we're really talking ancient history, Pete. That labor dispute was way back in '87. I know because I rode with old Pear against more damned drunken Texas cowhands than I ever want to see in one place again! There was nothing mysterious about the Hash Knife War, damn it. The Aztec Land and Cattle Company wanted to cut down on overhead, when the beef boom busted, by laying off some riders. Said riders took the position that if they were out of work, the outfit was out of business. Most of the raiding and bushwacking took place south of the county line. When some of it spilled over into Pear's county, we saddled up and rode down to put a stop to the nonsense. That's all there was to it. We just busted a few

heads and mayhaps strung a few cow thieves up, un-
official, and things got peaceful as hell. The outfit is
still in business, down in the Tonto Basin. Any pur-
loined beef we let get away has long since arrived in
the heavenly pastures of long-dead cows."

Stringer caught the barkeep's eye and held up two
fingers as he said, "I know all about the Hash Knife
War. I once wrote a feature on it. Let's get back to
that more recent killing of . . . what did you say his
name was?"

Old Pete, if that was his name, said, "Tom Graham. Some said at the time it was Pear hisself who
blew old Tom away. But I never bought that. Pear
was too decent a lawman to do a thing like that, even
if I did vote against him last time."

The barkeep slid two shot glasses of rye with beer
chasers across the bar to Stringer. He didn't care. It
was obvious Addams drank here more often. Stringer
took a polite sip of unasked-for rye, washed it down
with beer, and asked old Pete how come anyone
might have suspected Sheriff Owens of gunning a
suspect so informal.

Addams protested, "He never, and it was way
back in '92, damn it!"

Old Pete said, "Was it that long ago? Lord have
mercy, how time do fly once a man get's my age. I
never said Pear done it. The reason some said he
might have was that even earlier he'd run Tom Graham and all the others out of Pleasant Valley. You've
heard of the Pleasant Valley War, haven't you, Son?"

Stringer nodded and said, "The name rings a bell.
I can't say I was there. You say Sheriff Owens was
mixed up in that one as well?"

Old Pete cackled and declared, "Mixed up in it, hell, he put an end to it by running off both sides.".

Addams said, "I told him I'd just sit that one out when he tore off across county lines again. So I don't know much about that fuss."

Old Pete said, "I do. It was a feud between the Tewksbury clan and the Grahams. The Tewksbury clan was half-bred sheep men. The Grahams was cow, and just as ornery. They shot hell out of each other and everyone else they could get a bead on until old Pear decided that if the sissy Mormon sheriff down that way wouldn't stop 'em, somebody had to. So he did. I was one of the very few deputies he took along, and Lord did we have fun. Old Pear read the riot act to both sides, and then we was free to gun anyone on either side who broke the peace after that. It was in all the papers. There was some stink about Pear's rough and ready views on simple justice. But he just went ahead and done what was just, until both outlaw clans had been wiped out or drove off. Some of the wiping took place right here in Holbrook. So I reckon that shows whether Pear had jurisdiction or not. He shot it out with the Blevins boys just outside of town. He'd already shot their old man, and so they was sore at him as well as fighting for the Graham faction. Lord, what a mess old Pear made of that cabin they was holed up in. He nailed four of 'em. One lived to go straight. Old Pear was good at re-forming wayward boys."

The old timer wet his whistle with more beer and continued, "That was about the end of the Pleasant Valley War. The disputed range stood empty quite a spell. Then Tom Graham wandered back to round up the herd he'd left behind in his haste to get out of

Pear's range, and six weeks later he was found dead as a cow turd down in Pleasant Valley. Lord have mercy, was it really back in '92? Seems like yesterday."

Lawyer Addams said, "Speak for yourself, Pete. Like I said, that's ancient history. I helped Pear win many an election after that, and not even the infernal Republicans ever brought the old fuss up again."

Stringer asked, "Who wound up with all that range, if both the sheep men and cow men were run off by Sheriff Owens?"

Addams signaled the barkeep for another round, including old Pete, before he said, "I've no idea. I guess we could look it up at the courthouse tomorrow, if you think it's important."

Old Pete said, "*I* know who owns Pleasant Valley now. Nobody. Neither side never claimed Pleasant Valley formal. They wasn't formal types. Old John Tewksbury never really married that squaw he bred all them ferocious sheep-herding sons with, and the Graham brothers wasn't ones of formal papers neither. That was what made things so lively down that way. Both clans held their land, overlapping, by old fashioned gun law. Or they did before more regular law, in the person of Pear Owens, caught up with 'em."

Stringer frowned and said, "You mean all that range, a range worth fighting over, is still just there, unclaimed?"

Old Pete nodded and said, "Some say it's haunted too. I takes that with a grain of salt though. It wasn't no haunt as put that rifle ball in old Tom Graham. The stories about spooky lights and such are likely just superstition. You know how Indians and Mexicans are about places where blood's been spilt."

Addams snorted in disgust and said, "I can tell you why that old battleground lies empty today. Most of Arizona is still empty and unclaimed. Speaking as a lawyer, I'd advise anyone out to settle in these parts to avoid parts that have been settled in the past by anyone. Why risk a disputed claim when there's so much wide open space to file on, starting fresh?"

Stringer said, "I wouldn't know. What's that deserted range like?"

Addams said, "Ride a mile outside of town in the morning. This whole area is marginal range, where it isn't pure desert."

Old Pete shook his head and said, "You wasn't riding with us, W.R. They never named that valley Pleasant because it was ugly. There's plenty of grass, and even firewood, along Cherry Creek. That's a creek as runs the whole length of the valley all year. It was and is good range. But your point that it ain't the only such range is well taken. I reckon between its distance from the rail line and its nasty reputation, it's just been left the way it was because nobody's been ambitious enough to bother."

Stringer said, "I'd like to take a look at that old battleground. Is it far from here?"

They both nodded and Addams said, "Too far for a casual stroll. I make it a good fifty miles, wouldn't you, Pete?"

The older man nodded and said, "Fifty at least, with a lot of mighty rugged country between. Nobody could walk her this time of the year. A man would have enough of a chore getting down there with a pony and pack mule in, say, three or more days of mighty serious riding. The trail winds about, getting over some rimrock and a hell of a lot of white-hot sand. I'd forget it if I was you, son. It's a long rugged ride at any time of the year, and a total bitch in high summer. Worse yet, there's nothing much there when you get there, unless you believe in haunts."

Stringer smiled thinly and said, "I used to like to explore haunted houses when I was a kid."

Old Pete said, "We all did. But there ain't no house left, down yonder. Both sides got burnt out as well as shot up before the Pleasant Valley War was over."

Lawyer Addams added, "Anyone who'd be down there now would be more likely a stray Indian or an even less friendly outlaw seeking solitude. Pete's right about the valley's sinister rep. We might be able to scout up some adventurous youths to ride along with you if you just can't stand not going. But it's my duty as your attorney of record to warn you not to go alone."

Stringer didn't answer. He'd been brought up not to argue with his elders when he didn't have to. The notion sounded sort of dumb to him as well. But he'd already made up his mind that if he survived a whole night with old Madge, he'd just head down that way come morning.

CHAPTER
FIVE

He did. Old Madge said it had been a night she'd never forget, either, and Sam Barca, bless his crusty heart, had wired the money for the useless Chinatown feature via night-letter rates.

Stringer believed in traveling light. So he hired two tough-looking cow ponies and a center-fire saddle at the livery stable. One was a barrel-headed buckskin gelding, and the other a friskier paint mare. He meant to pack most of what he might need on the trail aboard his saddle and let the spare mount tag along free of care until he needed a fresh brute. The water bags he picked up at the general store figured to stay aboard the spare mount without a clumsy pack saddle he'd have to mess with. He bought a gunny of oats for the ponies and some trail grub he could eat cold, save for the coffee, of course. He hadn't brought a saddle gun along from Frisco. So he picked up an Army surplus Krag .30-30. When the shopkeeper tried to sell him a Winchester instead, he said he was more interested in accuracy than rapid fire on wide open desert or semidesert range. A sword bayonet came with the Army rifle. Stringer started to tell the shop keeper not to be silly. But as long as the deal cost the same either way, he decided to pack the wicked blade along. He'd discovered in Cuba that a Krag bayonet was good for opening cans or splitting kindling.

He was well on his way before nine, riding the paint and leading the buckskin. It only took a few minutes to ride clear of a town the size of Holbrook, and the day was shaping up as pleasant. The thin dry air of the Colorado Plateau was making short work of yesterday's unseasonable rain, but to do so, it had to cool some. There were still puddles here and there in the deeper ruts of the wagon trace he was following, and the overgrazed range this close to the tracks would no doubt green up a mite by the time he got back this way again. But otherwise the view was uninteresting.

Had he been riding north he'd have been entering the Painted Desert. Had he had any reason to ride east, he'd have been headed into the Petrified Forest, if one wanted to call a mess of stone logs stretched flat in the dust a forest. But this particular mess of nothing just lay gray and mostly flat as far as the eye could see. The cactus desert Arizona Territory was so famous for, lay miles to the south. There wasn't even a cow in sight, considering this was supposed to be cow country, and he seemed to have the wagon trace across it all to himself this morning.

He did, at least, until an hour out of town he heard hoofbeats behind him and turned in the saddle to see a gal chasing him at full gallop, sidesaddle. As she waved, he reined in, wondering why. He'd already told old Madge she couldn't come along.

It wasn't Madge. It was Patty Stern from the law office. She sure sat a horse well, he thought, and the palomino she was riding was almost the same shade of blond. She was wearing a whipcord riding habit and a dinky little derby that had to be pinned on good. As she slid her palomino to a stop she said, "I was so afraid I'd miss you. You should have dropped by the office before you left. That horrid woman at your hotel said she didn't know where you'd gone. But fortunately they were able to tell me at the livery."

He raised an eyebrow and observed, "You must have wanted to catch up with me bad. I thought all that trouble about Blue Streak had been settled, at least as far as I was concerned."

She said, "That's not why I rode after you. Are you really on your way to Pleasant Valley?"

He said, "I am, if I don't get lost. They told me I just have to follow this trail to the Pink Cliffs and west to a creek they call Chevelon."

She reached in her saddle bag as she said, "I brought you a map and some other things you might find useful."

As she handed over a well-stuffed manila envelope, she explained, "I dug all I could about the Pleasant Valley War out of the old county records. Carbons, of course. You may find some pages hard to read, and I fear they may be incomplete. You see, the county lines have been redrawn more than once in recent years, and Holbrook wasn't always the county seat. They may have more records on file

over at Saint Johns. When this country was less settled, it was all one monstrous county, and—"

"They told me Sheriff Owens was casual about
jurisdiction," he cut in, taking the envelope with a
nod of thanks and putting it in his own saddle bag.
He added, "I didn't think to bring any other reading
material, so I'm sure grateful, whether there's anything here I can use or not. Was this your own neighborly notion or did Lawyer Addams send you after
me?"

She said, "A little of both. It was my idea to look
through the county files. When I told W.R. I'd found
a few items that might be of interest to you, he
thought it was a good idea too. I wish I could get you
to read them now. It might save you a long dull ride
to nowhere."

He smiled crookedly and said, "I'm not headed
for nowhere. I'm going to have a look-see at Pleasant
Valley. But I'm all ears if you can tell me a better
place to go."

She sighed and said, "I read everything I dug out
for you, of course. Frankly, I found the old charges
and countercharges depressing. Both the warring
clans were trash whites who just seemed to enjoy
fighting. The point is that I saw nothing mysterious
or even new about that long-dead feud. Neither a
Graham nor a Tewksbury is likely to be anywhere
near Pleasant Valley now. Sheriff Owens hasn't been
down that way for almost ten years. He'd have surely
said so, if he thought there was a hidden treasure or a
gold mine, wouldn't he?"

Stringer shrugged and told her, "I can't say. I
came all this way to interview him, and found him
missing. Since nobody can tell me where he is, and

somebody else doesn't seem to want me to talk to him, anyway, all I can do is follow his footsteps in the hope of stumbling over whatever in thunder they don't want Owens to tell me."

She shook her head and said, "You're not being logical. Can't you get it through your head that the Pleasant Valley War ended a good ten years or more before Pear lost that recent election?"

Stringer said, "I can count. There's nothing mysterious about the last few years of his career. For one thing, he hadn't done much. What he did do is well documented, in and about the county seat. Nobody would have reason to gun me over a matter of common knowledge. So it has to be over something Owens did, or saw, well away from civilization."

"Some crimes he never reported?" She asked with a frown.

He shook his head and said, "Not if he was the sort of lawman everyone who knows him says he is. But with all due respect to a rough-and-ready old cuss, he might not have recorded what he might not have thought important at the time."

She sighed and said, "I wish you'd read those carbons I just gave you. Between the Pleasant Valley and Hash Knife wars, Pear and his deputies rode all over the Tonto Basin."

He nodded and said, "That's why I'm headed there."

She protested, "You must like to ride, then. We're talking about hundreds of square miles!"

He said, "I know. That's why I'd best get on down the road. It's been nice talking to you, Miss Patty."

She called him a fool again, wished him luck, and turned back. They hadn't been parted long before he

sort of missed her, not so much because of her trim
figure—although that was something to feel a mite
wistful about as well—but because the dull gray
open range all about looked lonesome as hell. As the
sun rose higher, even the lizards stopped amusing
him by trying to spook his paint.

He cheered up some when they topped a gentle
rise and he saw what had to be the pink cliffs they'd
told him about. He figured they had to be no more
than four or five miles off, keeping in mind how
desert air could fool human eyes. He stopped to
water and swap his ponies. He was glad he had, a
quarter mile on, when a snake or a mighty big grasshopper buzzed at them from a clump of trailside
yucca. The buckskin was steadier than the paint. It
just cocked one ear at the buzzing and plodded on.

Stringer made a mental note, in case he ever had
to fire a gun aboard either pony. He didn't want to
when he spooked a pair of wild burro a few miles on.
Wild burro knew they were considered good eating
as well as range pests. So they lit out to the west
cussing him in jackass as he laughed. There was a
haze of dust stirred up by other hooves in the direction they were running. Most range stock grazed un-
tended at this time of the year.

For once things viewed through thin dry desert air
were not much farther off then they looked. By mid-
afternoon he was following the old wagon trace west,
with the pink cliffs looming to his left. The eroded
escarpment rose more salmon than baby pink, but the
color was close enough, and whoever'd run all those
wagon wheels this way ahead of him had no doubt
known where they were headed. Going straight up
those rocks would have been a chore in any case.

The break in the cliffs, where Chevelon Creek punched through to flow north to the Little Colorado, was said to be about six or eight more miles. They'd make it easy before sundown, and see how far up the creek they could get before it was time to call it a day.

But they'd only gone three or four before Stringer began to have second thoughts about this whole deal. The afternoon sun was shining in his face now and not getting any cooler as it worked its weary way west in a cloudless cobalt sky. He told himself it would set and things would cool off soon. But another part of him asked, Then what? Come morning, we won't be a quarter of the way there, and tomorrow has to be hotter than it was today.

He told himself to shut up. But the more he rode, the more he thought, and it wasn't as if he knew there was anything ahead but more of the same. The notion that Pleasant Valley held some deep dark secret nobody local had noticed for a good ten years had made a lot more sense in the Bucket of Blood than aboard a pony, inhaling dust for hours. The late Blue Streak Bendix hadn't tried to run anyone out of Pleasant Valley, where nobody lived any more. He'd wanted a nosy reporter out of Holbrook, which was still full of folk, many of them from the old days and any one of whom might have learned anything the missing sheriff might know.

Stringer rode on a ways, wondering more and more just what he thought he was doing. He saw no break in the cliffs ahead. He thought about beer, and old Madge's bed. Then he muttered aloud, "Hell, the farther I am from town when I finally decide to turn back, the farther back I'll have to ride. And it's not as I had more than a half-assed hunch to follow all that tedious way."

Stringer was a man who took his time making up his mind, but once having done so, acted directly. So the first shot went wide when he'd simply reined in and swung his mount around on its hind hooves. As the second shot sizzled past him, closer, Stringer threw himself out of the saddle, drawing the Krag from its saddle boot as he did so, and landed in the dust on his shoulder.

He rolled behind a trailside clump of prickly pear that wasn't near as substantial as he'd have chosen, if there'd been time to make a choice. His spooked ponies ran off as the bushwacker fired a third time and spattered pear pulp all over Stringer's Stetson. Stringer worked the bolt of his Krag and fired back at the faint blue haze of gunsmoke he'd spotted among the salmon rocks near the top of the cliff in front of him. The rascal had obviously ridden along the flat top above to work down afoot into the eroded clefts of the rimrock. There was no easy way up from the trail Stringer had been riding. He fired again for luck as he licked his dusty lips and muttered, "Well, of course the son of a bitch has to know this country better. The question before the house is what's to be done now."

It was a good question. Stringer was pinned down good. He had reason to suspect he had his enemy in the same position, albeit the bastard was forted better. There was no way even a loco bushwhacker was going to charge down the cliff at him and reach the bottom alive. If he'd done enough, there was no way he could roll back over the rimrocks without outlining his fool self against the sky, and Stringer's Krag was sighted for well beyond that easy range. As if great minds were running in the same channels, the bushwhacker peppered Stringer's position with a fusilade of rapid fire. Stringer held his own fire as he watched the smoke drift off. He nodded grimly and said, "That was dumb. No long arm but a Winchester repeates that pronto, and so guess who's got the range on whom, even if you do have a mess of rocks to duck among up there."

He knew nobody with a lick of sense would stay put in one spot after firing, if he could help it. But he had no choice. So he knew his own best chance was to wait with a round in his chamber for a flash of hat or pants, then make it count.

Stringer craned his neck to see where his ponies might be now, if anywhere. He saw them a few hundred yards off, grazing. The lead rope, bless it, had hung up on a small stout bush, and once nobody had been shooting at them directly, they'd settled down. He could only hope the son of a bitch up yonder wouldn't think of the position he'd be in out here with two dead mounts.

As another .44-40 slug tore up the desert crust to his right, Stringer spoke as if his treacherous foe could hear, growling, "You know I could walk back from here if I had to. But you don't aim to give me the chance, right?"

As if in reply, the distant Winchester cursed him again, and again, the shot went a mite wide. Stringer knew that if the other exposed himself for a stand-up shootout, the Krag would have the best cards. Unfortunately, that other rascal seemed to know it.

Stringer got out the makings and proceeded to roll a smoke, one-handed as he muttered, "All right.

Who would have told them I was headed out this way
with a longer-ranging rifle?"

There were too many answers. He'd made no secret of his plans at either the livery or the general
store, and besides, he'd just pegged a .30-30 round
at the son of a bitch.

He licked the paper secure and lit the smoke. It
helped, even if his canteens were aboard that distant
buckskin. He hoped the rascal up above was feeling
thirsty by now. But, of course, if he'd planned all
this fun in advance, he'd likely brought his own canteen down over the edge with him. Stringer thought
about the way he'd been set up for the same fate as
the late Tom Graham, a few years back and farther
south. It was possible he was swapping shots with
the same disgusting gent. Stringer knew it was only
one he had to deal with. Had there been two or more,
they'd be trying to cross fire him by now. He nodded
and muttered,"Right. That dust off to the west before
was you, going lickety-split for the far end of that
cliff to get up top and into position for me. So it's
you and me alone out here, and ain't this fun?"

A Winchester round whizzed over his head.
Stringer knew the rising smoke from his roll-your-
own had drawn fire. He took a deep drag and tossed
the cigarette off to his left to smoke all it wanted over
there as he drew a bead on the last place he'd seen
smoke above him.

It only worked part way. His foe among the ruddy
rocks fired again after a time. But not from the same
spot. Stringer cursed and held his own fire, knowing
now that Swiss Cheese Cliffs had been the name
they'd been groping for way back when.

But the so-called pink cliffs were getting ever pinker as the sun kept sinking in the western sky. He could now make out the glow as well as the rising smoke from his cast-away cigarette as the shadows across the desert crust grew longer and more purple. He rolled over more, to pick out a man-sized clump of ungrazed cheat grass about as far from him as he was from the sniper up above. He knew that when he could no longer make it out, there was a good chance he'd be invisible from up there as well.

Meanwhile there was nothing much either could do but wait. So Stringer and no doubt the polecat up above got to enjoy one of the slowest sunsets either remembered. The first stars were winking in a now purple sky, and bats were flittering out of the rock clefts to confuse the issue further, when Stringer tried a lit match, flung wide, and nothing happened.

He started easing back, rose to his feet when he'd worked them into that cheat grass, and finally found his ponies in the dark.

As he watered them and changed the saddle back to the paint, he told them, "I reckon we won't be headed back to town, after all. I suspect that bastard left you both alive so I might, if he failed to cure my curious nature entire."

He remounted, staring up at the now black and featureless rock wall as he nodded and growled, "There must be something someone doesn't want me to see on that haunted range to the south, if they went to all that trouble to keep me from getting there. So I'm sorry, pards, but that's where we're going for sure now."

* * *

It was easy enough to find Chevelon Creek in the dark. For thanks to that recent rain, it was growling like it thought it was a river. By this time the moon was up, glinting on the white water of the creek and painting the wagon trace dull silver.

Stringer knew horses could see even better in the dark, and as long as one could see at all, crossing country like this by night had daylight riding under the hot sun beat. So though both ponies were tired and Stringer wasn't feeling so hot himself, he pushed on, planning to camp by moonset, anywhere along the handy water of the trailside creek.

He was getting sort of tired of waiting for the moon to set, too, by the time they got to the best campsite he'd seen since leaving Holbrook. It was a willow-hedged hollow between the creek and the wagon trace. The bottom of the bowl lay above the flood line, but just enough to hold grass and sedge, still edible, this late in the year. By the moonlight left, Stringer rubbed down both ponies, gave them each plenty of water and a few handfuls of oats, and left them hobbled to graze, knowing neither would stray from such a horse heaven, hobbled or not.

He built a small fire and spread his bedroll in the nearby grass as he waited for his coffeepot to boil. Then he made a few more basic arrangements for the night and left the fire to burn down to coals as he enjoyed his late snack of cold pork and beans up the slope, with his back against a black-willow trunk and the Krag across his lap.

He didn't light an after-supper smoke. He craved one, but no matter what old Madge had said the night before, he was a man who could control his desires when he thought he might have to.

It got quiet as the campfire burned down to glowing embers and the ponies settled down. When an owl hooted in its own tree across the clearing, Stringer perked up and quietly put his tin coffee cup aside in the grass. Owls sometimes did that for no sensible reason. But this time, after some time, he heard the cautious crunch of a boot heel on trail gravel.

There was nothing to be done about it just now. So Stringer just lay low like the tar baby until, sure enough, a figure moved between him and the ruby embers of the cook fire, eight or ten yards off. As the rascal pointed his own rifle at the sleeping Stringer he thought was under that fluffed-up bedding, Stringer told him, in a conversational tone, "Don't gun my bedding. Just drop that Winchester and turn around with some stars in your hands, friend."

The other man did no such thing. So Stringer shot him before he could swing the muzzle of that Winchester far enough to worry more about, and the rifle ball pitchforked its human target sideways into the campfire. As Stringer rose he expected to see the cuss at least try to roll off the hot coals. But he didn't, so Stringer had to kick him out of the fire as his duds started flaming and the clearing was filled with the sickly sweet reek of human flesh.

Stringer swore and scooped up the nearby coffeepot to pour over the sprawled man. The coffee was still hot, but he didn't seem to mind, and it kept his shirt from burning off him entirely. Stringer kicked the fire higher to have a look at what he'd just done. He could see at a glance the rascal was stone dead as

well as toasted. He was dressed cow style and still
needed a shave, despite the singeing. He was about
forty years old at the time of his recent death, and
Stringer was sure he'd have remembered such an
ugly face if he'd ever seen it before.

Stringer picked up the fallen man's Winchester
and sniffed it. He nodded and told the still form at
his feet, "Fired a lot, not long ago, and if you'd
come in a bunch, we might not be holding this conversation."

He hunkered down to go through the dead man's
scorched duds and found a cheap old watch and jack-
knife he had no use for. He put the fifty-odd dollars
and change in his own pocket, which seemed only
fair now. There was no I.D. of any kind on the mysterious son of a bitch. Stringer nodded and muttered,
"All right, you look mean and shabby enough to gun
a man for fifty bucks. So I shall assume the mastermind who's too yellow to come after me personal got
you out from under the same wet rock as old Blue
Streak."

The shabby stranger wasn't wearing a gun rig.
Stringer put his own rifle aside and picked up the
dead man's booted ankles to start hauling him away
from the fire, and it occurred to him that the murderous cuss hadn't wanted to be caught with the .38
he'd used on Blue Streak Bendix back at the town
clinic.

He dragged the limp form as far as the creek bank
and kicked it over the edge into the churning water,
saying, "Adios, you poor bastard. Give my regards
to your pals when you get downstream to 'em. I
wouldn't want 'em thinking you'd got lost in the desert."

As the body vanished, he turned back to look for its earlier means of transportation. He found a mal-treated chestnut tethered a hundred yards down the trail. The saddle was older and even more beat-up than the pony. There was no bedroll. He nodded knowingly. He hadn't figured the hired gun had planned a long trip. He unsaddled the spent pony and struck a match to see if he could spot a brand. He did. A plain U.S. branded on one shoulder. It was Army surplus, bought cheap by almost anyone off the remount service. He removed the bridle, patted the old horse reassuringly and told it, "Well, you're free to head on home or join my ponies for some free grass. You're no use to me either way."

The chestnut followed him back to his campsite. By now the fire was all the way out. Stringer left the dead man's mount to its own devices and hauled his bedding up into the willows for some shut-eye. He figured with three ponies and an owl to watch for further disturbances, he could safely catch a few winks. So he did, and it seemed no time at all before a lizard was trying to crawl in his ear and the morn-ing sun was trying to burn through his eyelids. So he sat up, cussing, to face another day. He knew it wasn't going to be any cooler than the one before. But now that he knew, for sure, that someone didn't want him anywhere near Pleasant Valley, it promised to be at least more interesting.

CHAPTER
SIX

Nothing happened. He rode most of the day, holing up in some rocks during the hottest part of the afternoon, but the only thing that seemed to be following him was that dead gun slick's old Army mount. He had to oat and water it each time he took care of the brutes he had more use for, of course. That was doubtless why it kept tagging along like an infernal pup. This wasn't good mustang country, even if the poor old critter had wanted to go wild in its declining years. He decided after cussing it some that it was just as well, for as he studied the map Patty had given him, he saw the creek he'd shoved the body in wouldn't take it back to Holbrook or anywhere near it. If the dead man didn't wash ashore at, say, Winslow, it was bound for the depths of the Grand Canyon. He hadn't worried about it, at the time, assuming the rascal's mount would return to Holbrook without him to alert his pals to the obvious. But if they didn't ever see him or his pony again, they might just assume he was still up to no good, and as long as they thought that, they might not send anyone else out to finish the job. There was a good chance the hired gun had made the deal to hit-and-run, without reporting back. Meanwhile, just in case he was being optimistic, Stringer worked to put more distance between himself and whomsoever.

He pushed on after sunset as far as the moon would let him, and nothing happened the next time he made camp, dry, on the edge of the Mogollon Rim.

That was about as high and dry as the Colorado Plateau got. The whole huge mass of high dry rock slanted gently mostly from where it had been thrust up from wherever with a considerable drop-off to the south. The Tonto Basin below the Mogollon Rim hadn't gone anywhere when the Colorado Plateau moved up in the world. So the drainage from the rim south ran into the Salt River to eventually join the Gila on its way to the Sea of Cortez or the Gulf of California, depending on one's mother tongue.

Not wanting to risk the steep descent in the dark, Stringer camped well off the trail until morning, and as he rode on by the dawn's early light, he was glad. The Mogollon Rim wasn't a sheer cliff everywhere, but it was still one hell of a drop, even where the trail hairpinned down it. Staring south, it made Stringer feel he was up in a balloon instead of a saddle. He knew there were other hills, far off across the big basin. He could even see some far below, sort of dividing the headwaters of two winding streams of white water, or at the distance, gray hairs. After winding down a tedious ways he saw the main trail trended to the basin to the west, and the map said that was the wrong way. So when he found what seemed more a deer path forking off to the east, he followed it. A good spell later he found himself following a babbling brook running on down through stirrup-high, albeit summer-dried, grass. He decided that if he wasn't in or close to Pleasant Valley, he'd sure found one that fit the name.

The nameless brook he was following, neither mapped nor likely running when it hadn't rained recently, ran in to join another, then another, until he reined in to compare Patty's map with the fair-sized creek forming up about here. There were what looked like charred ruins among the willows and cottonwoods a ways upstream. He rode up to them, leading the paint, with the old Army mount trailing on its own. As he reined in between the burnt-out homespread and the creek, he nodded and told his buckskin, "This has to be the Tewksbury place. Legend would have it that old Indian John and his squaw settled at the headwaters of Cherry Creek, and that's where we have to be at right now."

He dismounted to poke about among the ruins. There wasn't much to see. Earlier arrivals had even salvaged such hinges and other hardware the fire had left. Most of the light ash had long since blown away, and a lush bed of wild mustard had replaced any flooring the place had ever had. It made Stringer feel sorry for the old gal, at least, who'd once kept house here. It had no doubt been a step up in the world for an Indian gal. He wondered what nation she'd been begged, bought, or stolen from. He knew the Tonto Basin just over the rise to the west had gotten it's name from the so called Tonto Indians. Tonto meant stupid, in Mexican. It hardly seemed likely they'd called themselves that.

He went back out to the weed-grown dooryard and unloaded the ponies, saying, "You brutes go on and graze in this nice shade for now. The sun's getting high again, and now that we're here, I'm in no rush. I mean to study this place good before we go on down to see what the Grahams might have left behind in their haste to leave this valley."

He fed himself as well, seated on the charred sill of the old abandoned house to polish off more beans, washed down with a can of tomato preserves. He didn't build a fire to make coffee this time. Even in the shade it was too damned hot.

As he rolled a smoke later, he decided the old squaw man and his woman could have picked a worse place to raise sons and sheep. It was warmer down here than up above the Mogollon Rim. But the valley was well watered and the grass all around grew lush as hell for Arizona Territory. There was plenty of firewood, and in season no doubt wild cherries, if the name they'd given the creek meant anything at all. It seemed a shame they'd lost it all. He rose, got the carbon papers from his saddle bag, and sat back down to see if they could offer a more sensible explanation than the legends about two half-witted white-trash clans just killing one another off for the hell of it.

They didn't. As he read through the old county records, he was sort of glad he'd waited. For although he knew now that he had to be on to something, had he read all this nonsense sooner, he'd never ridden down here, nobody would have tried to stop him, and he'd have no story at all for old Sam Barca.

He didn't have to take notes, since he knew he

could just as easily carry all this confusion back to
Frisco with him, when and if he ever figured a story
angle out for his paper.

The various county clerks of various counties
who'd compiled all this disconnected stuff about
Sheriff Owens and all the folk he'd had trouble with,
had certainly not been writers with any sense of plot.
Stringer could see Patty had picked out only the old
records the sheriff appeared in. He knew she'd done
so to help him. Had he had her here to fuss at, he'd
have told her never to do that to a newspaper man.
To research old records right, a man needed all the
records, damn it. This hodge-podge, while as exciting as many a penny dreadful, only told him that in
his day old Commodore Perry Owens had been a
pisser.

There were charges and countercharges about a lot
of long-gone gents of Anglo, Mex, and Indian persuasion who'd tried to treat old Pear mean and
wound up getting treated meaner. Stringer had to
allow that on more than one occasion the hard-cased
peace officer had kept the peace way the hell outside
his jurisdiction. But while he seemed to take the atti-
tude that any no-good rascal he could get at no doubt
deserved some taming, even his enemies had been
unable to tar Owens with either cowardly or need-
lessly cruel behavior. Stringer got so confused trying
to sort out where on earth what county's line had
been drawn, as they sort of shifted them about and
even renamed them to include or exclude certain vot-
ing cliques, that he tended to forgive old Owens for
not paying much attention to such petty details. This
valley had for certain never been part of Navajo,
Apache, or whatever county the old lawman had

been elected to police. On the other hand, the county seat of Globe was south of the Salt, and from the records, hadn't been too interested in shootouts up this way. So old Pear had done what he'd no doubt thought he had to do, and here it was, years later, and what in thunder was so secret about this valley, out of the way as it might be?

He looked up as he heard hoofbeats. He stood up, stuffing the papers in a hip pocket to free his gun as he saw what was coming his way.

There were four of them, dressed cow and loaded for bear. But there was nothing sneaky about their approach. So Stringer just waited, smiling curiously as they rode in, reined to a stop, and one of them demanded to know who the hell he thought he was and what he was doing there.

Stringer said, "You can call me Stringer MacKail. I ride for the *San Francisco Sun*. I'm here because my editor wants a feature on the Pleasant Valley War."

The obvious leader—a lean, hungry-looking individual with a hatchet face and eyes to match— laughed in surprise and told Stringer he was a mite late, adding, "The last of the Grahams got kilt back in '92. September, they say. I wasn't here. I'm called Montana Mason. We all ride for the Hash Knife. You don't. Let's talk about why you're really here. I could say I writ for *The New York Times*. But that wouldn't make it true."

Stringer nodded and said, "I am reaching, polite, for my press pass. I'll allow it could be a forgery. But you'll have to allow that would be a lot of trouble for even a cow thief to go to. I also stand ready to let you search my saddle bags for running irons, if that's what all this is about. No offense, but aren't you boys a mite off your own range if you're searching for missing stock?"

Montana reached down for the credentials as he said, "If the damned cows were on our range they wouldn't be missing, would they?"

He read the press pass, handed it back, and said, grudgingly, "You ain't packing a throw rope on yon saddle, and them damned old cows are most often found in the company of Mexicans these days. We're missing eight head. Have you seen 'em?"

Stringer said, "I haven't seen cow one since I came over the rim this morning. What makes you suspicious they could be over in this valley?"

Montana said, "The greasers. Not the greasers as stole our stock. The ones as say this valley is inhabited by spooks. We don't believe in spooks. But you can see for yourself what a handy place this would be to keep cows."

Stringer said he sure could, but added, "It's my understanding this range has been abandoned."

Montana snorted in disgust and said, "That's what I just said. There's grass and water, and no law-abiding folk for miles. The greasers say that there's even wild cows in parts of this valley. Wild horses too. The coyotes got all the sheep long ago, but nobody ever rounded up the last of Tom Graham's herd, years ago."

Stringer gazed about and said, "Well, feel free to round up all the stock you see, branded or otherwise. If it was a herd worth fighting over, someone would have surely claimed it long before this, right?"

Montana said, "Ain't looking for mavericks. Looking for Hash Knife beef. We don't hold with wild Texas views on the ownership of stock. The outfit treats us decent, and we try to act the same."

Stringer nodded and said, "I heard that was what the Hash Knife War was all about. I take it you boys rode for the winning side."

It had been a statement rather than a question. But all four of them laughed incredulously. Then Montana asked, "Jesus H. Kee-rist, do I look dumb enough to have rid that long without making it to a desk position with the company? You're talking about a fight back in '86 or '7, pilgrim. None of us had rid for the outfit half that long."

Another Hash Knife rider chimed in, "They'd run all the sheep out of the Tonto by the time they hired us. There ain't been any kind of war in these parts for years."

Montana growled, "We'll see about that when we catch up with them cows and any sons of bitches keeping them company. Let's go, boys."

Stringer said, "Wait. Where do I find these Mexicans who say this range is haunted?"

Montana shrugged and said, "Anywhere but on it, of course. Any fool can see how free from care the grass all around has growed."

Another rider with a kinder face, an easy thing to manage, told Stringer, "Us white riders don't get over this way much because our own Tonto Creek runs twenty miles or more from this one, with some mighty dry range between. The desert due east is worse. You know about the rimrock country to the north."

"Then new settlers would tend to drift in from the Mormon-Mex country to the south?"

"They might, if the spooks would let 'em. I've

never seen a spook my ownself. Like I said, we don't get over this way much."

Montana snapped, "You'll *be* a spook if you don't do as I say, and I just said let's go, damn it!"

The four of them rode off down Cherry Creek as Stringer sort of wondered why. It wasn't his business to recover beef for the Aztec Land and Cattle Company. But had they been more polite, he could have given them some helpful hints on the subject.

He knew Montana was younger, or dumber, than he looked.

That was fair. In a restless land of opportunity the day had not yet dawned when a man with any imagination would grow old herding someone else's beef. But Stringer had been a top hand in his own misspent youth, so he could have told them any cow thief with a lick of sense would know better than to run stolen stock down the watered center of a wide-open valley.

As he tossed his spent smoke down and ground it out with a boot heel, Stringer gazed professionally at the distant skyline to his east. They'd said the country over that way was more rugged. A smart thief trying to work stolen stock south to the nearest market would hold them by day in some dry wash and let them graze and water down this way by night. Cherry Creek ran all the way to the Salt, a hell of a ways farther than it would pay the Hash Knife to search for property of finite value. Those four riders, useless or not, had to be costing the outfit five dollars or more a day, and they couldn't be the only Hash Knife parties out searching for said beef. So, yeah, they'd give up once they'd followed the creek say a day's ride each way.

Meanwhile they were out of sight now, and he

didn't see how a few head run off so recent could have anything to do with the secret someone else didn't want printed in the newspapers. So he got to work on the old Tewksbury home spread.

By mid-afternoon he'd worked his way out of ideas as well as shade, having started from the middle by prying up the old hearthstone and finding nothing but mormon-cricket grubs under it.

Buried treasure made no sense. The secretive mastermind who kept sending hired guns after curious strangers had had over ten years to dig up anything of value the long-gone half-breed clan could have ever left in these parts. But Stringer made sure anyway. He even dug into a suspicious low spot out back, still soft from the recent rain, until his nose warned him he was probing into the sanitary habits of a large and mighty stinky family, considering how long it had been since anyone could have stepped out back to the shithouse.

Other low spots figured to be garbage pits or previous positions of the portable squat-and-drop. He found one deeper and more open crater among the weeds, where some earlier explorer had made sure of his or her suspicions by excavating a mess of busted crockery, glass, and animal bones. Mostly sheep and at least one pig. Stringer wondered why they'd dug just there and not anywhere else. He decided that someone who'd once visited the spread when it had still been inhabited would know where the shithouse and more recent garbage pits had been. The place they had dug showed they'd given up just a few feet down. It hardly seemed likely the Tewksbury family plate had been buried shallow, mixed with after-dinner scraps. So the earlier treasure hunters hadn't been too serious. Perhaps, like himself, they'd simply wondered what all the fuss had been about down this way.

As the sun got lower and the sunny slopes all about began to at least *look* cooler, Stringer saddled the paint to ride on. He didn't want to camp too close to the burnt-out Tewksbury place.

Haunted or not, the scene was sort of depressing. The old Army mount must have thought so too, for even though there was now grass and water all about, the fool critter puppy-dogged after Stringer and his hired ponies. He warned it, "With virgin grass as lush as this free for the asking, you can just forget about oats in the near future, Army."

But the old chestnut followed them anyway. Stringer stayed near the stream running the length of the wide flat-bottomed valley. Unlike the Hash Knife riders who'd proceded him this way, he wasn't looking for stolen stock. He wanted to get the feel of this once hotly disputed range.

It was fine range now. Thanks to that recent rain the tall tawny grass was already starting to green at the roots again, and the sedge along the creek stayed green all the time in any case. There was more nutrition in the grass, even dry. But sedge made a nice sort of salad for stock, and save for a nibble here and again, he could see neither grass nor sedge had been grazed in recent memory. So much for the legend of abandoned herds. At the most a burro here and a desert bighorn there might account for the very few signs of any grazing at all. Wild critters tended to graze on the run like that. It hardly seemed possible anyone was holding enough stolen beef down this way to matter. So that couldn't be the secret.

As he rode at an easy walk toward the old Graham spread his map said he'd find farther down, he tried to picture this range as it might have looked back in the days blood was spilled over it. The grass would have been a lot shorter, of course, and the gentle slopes all around would have been dotted with cows and sheep, albeit hardly at the same time and place.

Stringer had been raised cow, so he'd naturally grown up on the horror stories cattlemen told about sheep. Having seen more of the world since, he'd learned that while sheep and cattle had their differences, human greed caused more trouble than either sheep or cow men liked to admit.

It was true that sheep could manage on range too overgrazed for cow, and that once they had to forage seriously, sheep could ruin what was left of a range by digging for roots with their buck teeth and sharper little hooves. But back east and all over Australia, cows and sheep were grazed together in mixed herds by cooler heads who knew when it was time to move on and give any range a rest.

On well-managed range, sheep and cattle grazed more efficiently together than either species could graze alone. Unless driven by hunger and dearth, cows preferred grass, and having no front teeth, didn't mow it down to the roots. Sheep could, and would, if they had to. But left to their druthers, sheep preferred broad-leafed forbes the cows tended to ignore if there was grass enough to matter. In a mixed herd the cows kept the grass from choking out the weeds while the sheep kept the weeds from choking out the grass. On overgrazed range, of course, all bets were off. You could tell overgrazed cattle range by its scattered welcome mats of close-cropped grass surrounded by tough chaparral and haunted by tumbleweed. You could tell overgrazed sheep range by bare ground and gullies. Neither seemed a problem in these parts this afternoon. The healing grass had filled in a gully here and there. But apparently the Graham faction had shot off the Tewksbury clan before their sheep had done much damage.

Stringer reconsidered one of the carbons Peggy Stern had let him have to ponder. Both sides had charged the other with every vice known to man, and some other locals had charged both with worse. It was a mite late to worry about now, but at one time it had been hinted by some that the war hadn't really been over sheep versus cattle. It was said that at one time the Graham and Tewksbury boys had ridden together, against Mexicans, of course. Along with some other Anglo hands they'd shot up the Hispanic fiesta of Saint John the Baptist in Saint John's, the original county seat east of Holbrook, named by the original Mexican settlers in these parts.

Sheriff Owens's part in the amusing event had been his preventing the outraged Mexicans from lynching an Anglo called Greer. The records were incomplete. So it was hard to say how Greer fit in with the later Graham-Tewksbury feud. Owens had run Dick Greer out of the county after a later discussion about sheep versus cattle with a Mexican sheep man who'd been slower on the draw. It had been charged by other Mexican sheep men that old Indian John Tewksbury had entered the sheep business at their expense, to the considerable annoyance of the Graham brothers, no matter how they might have felt about Mexicans.

But another version had it that their pal, Dick

Greer, had been a sheep man himself, and that the fuss with the Mexicans had been over range, not species. That made sense in a land where grass and water came scarce, no matter what you wanted to use it for.

Stringer dug the carbons from his hip pocket to refresh him memory, and yeah, there was the unsubstantiated rumor that the Graham and Tewksbury boys had together robbed the bank in Saint John's and later argued over the spoils, together with gossip to the effect a Graham had been caught in a hay loft with one of the Tewksbury women. No names were offered. But all of Indian John's grown sons had women, even if they had been sheep herders, and old Indian John had himself married up with an English immigrant gal named Lydia after his old squaw died. An old man with a new young wife likely would have felt mighty surly if he'd caught even a good pal messing with her.

Stringer decided that on the other hand the simple answer was most often the best one. Old Indian John and his brood had been here first. He might have welcomed new neighbors at first, if only as allies again the surrounding Mexican and the even older Indian element. But then the Grahams had brought in other Texas tribes called Simpson, Blevins, and such as their own allies, and there was a record showing old John Simpson had tried to buy the Tewksbury range, with the Grahams backing him when he accused Indian John of being no more than a squatter and a known cow thief.

Stringer put all the flimsy carbons in his saddle bag for now. They were only starting to confuse him more. Whatever the feud had started over, it had been a long nasty fight that both sides had lost in the end.

He spotted a lonesome chimney ahead, upslope a ways from the creek. That made sense. This far down Cherry Creek would flood its banks pretty good after a heavy rain. As he rode uphill to investigate the ruins, he spotted buzzards circling above the skyline far beyond the chimney. He wondered why. He set the thought aside while he poked about the abandoned site. It looked more salvaged than burned. The only hardware left was a horseshoe nail rusting on the long-cold hearthstone. Hardly any housewife let a horse doze by her cooking fire. Some later visitor had no doubt lost the nail, poking about in here aboard his pony long after the roof timbers had been carted away. There was nothing to say whether the folk who'd lived here had been named Graham or anything else, and the site wasn't on the map Patty had given him. Unless one of the Tewksbury boys had lived here with his own wife, it conflicted with old Indian John's claim, penciled and noted as such on the printed map.

As Stringer remounted he saw a column of flies hovering over one spot, just upslope, and rode over for a closer look. A cow pie, fairly dry now but still fresh enough to draw flies, winked up at him from the grass. He got out his makings and rolled a smoke as he stared up at the skyline and muttered, "Howdy, buzzards. You sure seem interested in something over yonder. There ain't supposed to be any stock on this range right now, but somehow I doubt that's a bird turd under all these flies down here."

He rode on up, spare and pet mount trailing, as he hauled out the Krag and worked the bolt before rest-ing it across his thighs behind the saddle swells, polite but ready.

This time the thin dry air sort of fooled him. For when he got to the top of the rise he saw the buzzards were hovering over yet another, rockier ridge to the east. He kept going, and sure enough, there was yet another rise ahead. It was getting tedious when he finally rode between two big boulders to see what the buzzards, now directly about him, were staring down at.

A half-dozen, no, exactly eight cows lay scattered not too far apart down the far slope. They hadn't been dead long enough to bloat. But buzzards didn't wait that long. There was a brush lean-to someone had thrown up between him and the dead stock. There was a dead fire near it as well. Stringer was still working it out when a bullet spanged off the boulder to his right, followed by a pistol report and a high-pitched voice cussing him just awful in Spanish.

Stringer yanked the reins and crawfished his mount back as he dismounted, rifle in hand, to belly flop in the tall grass between the boulders, yelling back, *"Qué pasa? Usted es todos parecen irritados por nada!"*

The girl in the lean-to detected his accent and shouted back in passable English, "Go away! I have a gun!"

Stringer called back, "I noticed. I've got one too. It's a rifle. If I meant you any serious harm, I'd be peppering that clump of weeds you're hiding in pretty good by now. So come on out and let's talk it over more civilized."

She pegged another pistol shot his way. He could see from her smoke she was hunkered low and aim-

ing through the brush at him. He sighted carefully
and sent a .30-30 round through the same, high
enough to keep from really parting her hair.

It worked. A nickel-plated Smith & Wesson sailed
into view to land in the grass at a safe distance. Then
the lady who'd been firing it at him, really a girl,
stepped into view with her hands in the air and a
defeated look on her pretty brown face. She was
dressed part Indian, too, in a maroon pueblo shirt
with a silver concho waistband, and a more His-
panic-looking calf-length campesina skirt which
might have been red before it was washed once too
often. He couldn't see her feet in the tall grass, but
her parted and braided black hair seldom went with
hight-button shoes.

He got to his own feet and moved down to join
her, his Krag lowered politely at his side. She was
even younger and prettier as he got closer. She licked
her lips and asked simply, "Are you going to kill me
or just rape me, señor?"

He smiled down at her and said, "I haven't made
my mind up yet. How come you seem so intent on
guarding them dead cows from the birdies up above?
Can't you see they're rapidly becoming unfit for
human consumption?"

She said, "They refuse to come down while anything here still lives. I am here because I have no
place better to go, thanks to your cruel friends,
señor."

He said, "I've been riding alone some time now.
When's the last time you've had water, señorita?"

She lowered her hands experimentally, saw he
didn't seem to mind, and pointed at her shelter, saying, "I have all our canteens and perhaps enough

food for two more days. But our mules all ran away when the shooting started last night. I ran away too. That is for why I am still alive. Papacito and Ramon were not fast enough. I buried them both where I found them, over there."

Stringer stared soberly at the two flimsy crosses fashioned from weed stems, and asked, "How did you manage? Do you have a shovel in that hut?"

She said, "With difficulty. The few camping tools we had departed with our mules. But the earth was not too hard, thanks to that rain the other day."

He nodded and said, "Well, I could try to put it all together by myself. I can see the running iron some-one left in that long-dead camp fire. But why don't you just tell me what in the hell took place up here?"

She suggested they get into the shade of her lean-to. They did. They sat on the one Navajo blanket she had, and he rolled a smoke for her as she told him her simple story.

Her name was Concepción. Her father and older brother had let her come along to cook for them as they'd ridden up this way from the Salt River Valley to check out the tales they'd heard of abandoned beef roaming free for the asking up this way.

He cut in to warn her, "We're not likely to get along as well if you fib too much, Concepción. I have it on good authority that the Hash Knife, to the west, is missing exactly eight head of stock, and no offense, I can read their brand on the rump of that nearest dead cow."

She shrugged and said, "We did not steal them. We found them grazing alone over by Cherry Creek. The Hash Knife ranges its beef along the Tonto, no?"

He sealed her smoke and lit it for her as he said,

"I reckon that ferocious thunderstorm the other day could have spooked a stray or more from one water-shed to another. But for folk who knew where the Hash Knife usually runs its stock, you must not read brands so good."

She took a deep sensuous drag on the smoke he'd given her before she replied, simply, "We are poor. All this land was ours before your people stole it from us, señor."

He shook his head and said, "We never stole it. We licked Mexico fair and square for it. Just like your folk licked the Indians for it to begin with. But save your excuses. I'm neither the law nor the proper owner of the stock you meant to reclaim as your birthright. Your menfolk herded them up here to run the brands whilst you tended to camp chores for 'em. What happened then?"

She said, "It was after dark. We had just eaten. Ramon was, it is true, poking his iron in the fire, as teenaged boys will. Our Papacito had said it would be best to wait for daylight so they could, ah, work more artistically on the brands of the orphaned stock we had rescued. I had to attend to a call of nature. So I moved up the slope, away from the firelight, for to do so. I had no sooner finished when the shooting started. I did not see who was shooting. We had no pistols with us. We were not that kind of people. I saw Ramon leap to his feet, then fall right down again. I heard someone shouting cruel things about Mexicans. As I was Mexican, I ran. I ran far, fearing each step would be my last. But I do not think they knew about me. Nobody chased me. I fell down in some thick grass and wept a long time. Then it was dawn, and oh so quiet. After a long time I crept back to our campsite to find it as you see it now, except for the bodies of my father and brother, buried up the slope. They must have been Hash Knife riders, no?"

He shook his had and said, "No. Two reasons. I just met some Hash Knife riders, well after sunrise. They were still searching for the stock. The second reason is that they weren't searching for their own stock to butcher it and leave it for the buzzards. Hash Knife riders might have treated your menfolk just as surly, but they'd have rounded up them eight cows and taken 'em home with 'em. So who's left, and how come I had to duck those pistol rounds if you innocent folk came all this way without pistols?"

She said, "I found the gun, loaded, in deep grass near poor Papacito. One of them must have dropped it in the dark, no?"

He said, "I'll know better in a minute," then crawled back out into the sun to look for the gun she'd tossed out there someplace. It only took him a few moments to recover it. It was a .38. He rejoined her and told her, "A man was murdered in Holbrook the other night. Someone might have thought he was stretching his luck by packing it after he'd shot your menfolk with it as well. Or, hell, it could be just one of those things. Either way, I can see I was wrong assuming there was only one hired gun prowling about down this way. It looks like they sent one after me and some others over this way to make sure I didn't find something out if I managed to get through."

She stared soberly at him to ask, "Then the same monsters who killed my father and brother are after you, as well, Americano?"

He said, "I am called Stuarto, by your kind, Con-

cepción. I can't say *why* we seem to have enemies in
common. But it's sure starting to look that way. Have
your people had trouble up this way before with
sneaky night riders?"

She let out some smoke and said, "Yes and no,
Stuarto. Fights between my people and your own do
not take place as often or as seriously as they might
have when this range was inhabited by most-rough
Anglo tribes. But my people tell tales of their ghosts
still riding their old range."

"Do you believe in ghosts, Concepción?" he
asked.

She shook her head and said, "No. Neither did
Papacito. He said the wild cattle still ranging up this
way were more like money on the hoof than a spiri-
tual matter. Alas, whatever does still haunt this range
proved him and my poor brother wrong!"

Stringer said, "Ghosts hardly ever use a nickle-
plated Smith and Wesson on a man. But tell me what
else your people say about spooks up here in Pleasant
Valley, as long as we're on the subject."

She said, "They tell all sorts of ghost stories about
this old battleground. Years ago, when the last of the
Grahams was run out by ferocious gringo sheriff,
both your kind of people and mine moved in for to
round up the abandoned herd and salvage the abandoned housing. It is said that when old Tom Graham
came back later, some squatter ambushed him for to
keep him from reclaiming the valley with all his old
enemies gone."

Stringer nodded and said, "That left the range
abandoned total. So what happened to the ones who
must have wanted to move in on such good grazing?
They say old Indian John defended his small part of

it at gun point. So he must have thought it worth something."

Concepción nodded and said, "It is said his ghost still values the land he died for. Perhaps he still fights the ghosts of his enemies for it. As you say, those mysterious riders who murdered my father and brother in the dark last night had no *human* reason to do so. Over the years many others have tried for to settle up this way. They, too, have always been driven out by whatever seems to be haunting this range. I do not know all the stories. I was very little when everyone decided it just wasn't wise to ride up this way after dark, or be here after the sun went down. There are tales of sheep being run over cliffs, and new homesteads burning down mysteriously. There are tales of livestock, and owners of livestock, simply vanishing forever, as if the spirit would have claimed them early."

She repressed a sob and added, "Oh, if only Papacito had not been so brave. What is to become of me now?"

He said, "I have a spare Army horse who may be delighted to meet you, Concepción. You're a lot smaller than the gents he's more used to carrying. You'll have to ride bareback. But that still beats walking. How far are we talking about?"

She smiled for the first time and said, "I have many people in the Sierra Apache, just south of the Salt, about thirty of your miles from here."

He nodded and said, "Well, I mean to take it slow and scout this valley good, but I'm headed that way, and that old Army mount seems to want to tag along in any case."

As he helped her out of the lean-to with her

meager belongings, he studied his mental map a bit more and added, "If you can get that old brute to part company with my paint and buckskin, you might be safer bee-lining on ahead of us. Like I said, I seem to have someone looking to gun me, and I ain't ready to run just yet."

She said, "I will feel safer traveling with you, and do not worry, Stuarto—my people dwell in the Sierra Apache, but they are mostly Papago, on the Indian side."

CHAPTER
SEVEN

It was good to have someone to talk to who wasn't a horse, and Concepción was helpful in other ways as they followed the now lower waters of Cherry Creek south together. She was able to save him some time by pointing out the abandoned ruins left by folk run out long after the warring clans had been gone; unless, as some said, they were still haunting their old disputed range.

By sunset he figured they were about a third of the way down Pleasant Valley, as Patty Stern's map defined the sort of undefined edges. The claim lines penciled across the map in the conflicting interests of the two warring factions overlapped a lot. He could see why they'd decided to settle it by gun law instead of in court, whichever court had jurisdiction this far from Holbrook and even farther from the former county seat at Saint John's. He made a mental note to ask for a look-see at the original claims filed by one and all, assuming there were still any on file and he got back alive.

Since that was beginning to look like a tedious chore, he told the pretty little Mex gal they'd be eating cold and camping with no fire, well upslope from the old trail they were following, once it got too dark for anyone ghosting them from the distant skyline to make out any direction they might want to turn.

She said she knew a good spot not far ahead. He said, "Anyone who's made a habit of haunting these parts any time at all will surely know all the good campsites. What we want is a campsite of no particular interest and a good field of fire all around it."

They didn't have long to wait before the sun went down, and since the moon hadn't risen yet, it got plenty dark. Stringer told her, "Right. To begin with, we want to go back at least a quarter mile before we ford the creek and mosey up the far side."

He expected her to ask why. But there was a lot to be said for riding with a sidekick who was part Papago. They were mighty slick Indians—one of the only other nations the Apache respected and, some said, feared.

The Papago were less famous than some less intelligent Indians. One had to be sort of stupid to take on the U.S. Army with a bow and arrow. The Papago had been desert hunters and part-time farmers in the old days, who'd just wanted to be left alone and were willing to return the favor. Apache, Navajo, and other such Dené-speaking breeds had been untidy neighbors for other Indians well before they'd learned other bad habits from the Mexicans and then the Anglos. So they'd been slaughtering Papago and vice versa long before anyone with a horse or gun had shown up to teach 'em how to do it right. The Papago had taken the position that nobody who fought Apache or Navajo could be all bad. Since they were having all the trouble they needed with the same enemies, the early Spanish and even sensible Americanos had been willing to treat the Papago decent, and pretty little gals like Concepción had resulted from the mutual admiration. Papago guides and scouts had helped rather than hindered wagontrains taking the southern route to California, and in return the whites had given the friendly Papago enough guns and ammunition to chase their Apache enemies well east of the Sierra Apache, no matter what the map might say.

After they'd doubled back on their trail a ways, Stringer led all his traveling companions across the creek and as far as a rise that offered nothing but an uphill charge to anyone else who meant to join them uninvited.

As Concepción spread their bedding on the dry grass, Stringer led the three ponies down the far slope and hobbled them good, saying, "No oats, and I'm sorry about the water. If any of you bust loose, we'll never speak to you again."

He moved back to the top of the isolated hill and asked the girl what she was doing in the dark, since it sounded funny. She said she was trying to open a damned old can. He sat down beside her and groped in his saddle bags until he found the bayonet that had come with his Army rifle. She thought it made a neat can opener. It was a little ominous, the way she sliced through tin with no fooling around. He was glad she didn't have Apache blood. They shared the beans. She said she'd never eaten frijoles half as sweet. He said he didn't like pork and beans cold either, but that he'd brought them along because they stuck to the ribs no matter what they tasted like.

She dug in her own leather sacks to produce some tortillas that might have tasted better with butter. They went just fine with the beans. They were still a mite hungry after sharing so little. He'd figured on washing it all down with tepid canteen water, but she produced an earthenware bottle of pulque. It tasted no worse than any other cactus juice, and had a mild kick to it. He knew that by the time you drank enough pulque to feel it, your mouth would taste soapy in the morning. So he just drank enough to be polite. Concepción asked if it was safe to smoke, and when he told her he didn't think so, she polished off the whole bottle.

The moon rose, big and orange as a pumpkin to the east. He hadn't noticed until then what she was wearing, or not wearing, as she sat cross-legged on her blanket with her duds fluffed up as a pillow near the head of what would have been a bed had it not been a Navajo blanket.

She stared off down the slope and said, "Oh, I can see almost as far as the creek now, Stuarto."

He said, "So can I. Don't you even pull a top cover over you when you bed down so, ah, informal?"

She said, "I have no top cover. Perhaps I shall wrap up in the one blanket I have. That is up to you, Stuarto."

He thought about that as he studied her by moonlight. The light wasn't good enough to stare deep in her big sloe eyes. What he could see was distracting as hell to a man who hadn't had any the night before. She was little as an Anglo twelve-year-old, but no man would ever mistake a gal with moonlit breasts as big and firm as hers for a child. She was sort of hairy for part Indian too.

He sighed and said, "Well, I'd have one hell of a time falling to sleep right now, even if it was midnight, which it ain't. But we have to settle on some ground rules here, Concepción. You know I like you too much to shoot you. But I know how your people feel about a love-'em-and-leave-'em Gringo too. So . . ."

She laughed and asked, "Madre de Dios, do you think I wish for to take you all the way home with me to meet my family?"

He said, "That might not be wise."

She said, "My cousin, Hernan, would try for to kill you, and I am fond of him too."

He tossed his hat aside in the grass and started to unbuckle his gun rig as he said, "I hope you understand that my job calls for me to travel a lot."

And then she was laughing like a mean little kid, and was all over him before he could get out of his shirt and jeans, let alone his boots. As she unbuttoned his pants, pulled them down just enough to be embarrassing, and impaled her wiry little body on the results, he laughed and said, "Wouldn't this make more sense if you let me undress entire and get on top?"

She moaned, "Ay, querido, do not tease me with romantico talk!"

She collapsed limply down on him leaving him way up indeed until he could roll her on her back to finish right. She liked it that way, too, and returned the favor by helping him undress further while in action. He didn't get the boots off until later, of

course. She wanted more. But he pulled one of his
own blankets over them and told her to hold the
thought, explaining, "It can't be ten o'clock yet and
it's starting to get cold as hell."

She snuggled closer, took the matter more firmly
in hand, and told him she knew great ways to keep
warm on a chill desert night.

He could see she did. He'd already learned that
rumba was just the Spanish word for a spree. But the
word took on a whole new meaning as she twisted
her trim hips in every direction at once and begged
for more. He didn't ask, so he'd never know how on
earth she'd learned so many interesting ways to move
her tawny little body. He knew she couldn't be more
than twenty-odd, and he knew that people here
tended to raise their girls rather strictly.

On the other hand, accepting her story at face
value, she'd come from the Salt River Valley to be
naughty, and the least a gent could do would be to
oblige. So he did, a lot, and between that and the
pulque it seemed to settle her nerves enough for them
to get some sleep by midnight.

She didn't let him sleep until dawn. He growled a
bit when he found himself half awake, chilled to the
bone, with her shaking him hard. He yawned and
said, "Jesus, doll, I don't know if I can right now."

But she said, "Stuarto, I think I just saw an *espec-
tro*!"

That woke him up. But as he sat higher to look
the way she was pointing in the dim light, there
seemed to be nothing to see. He said, "I thought we
agreed there were no ghosts, honey."

She said, "I saw it anyway. A pale green light,

down that way on the other side of the creek. As if it was signaling or searching for something."

He grimaced and said, "It was probably just someone with a railroad lantern. When they're not red they're often green. Some wiseass is trying to read our trail, I reckon."

She shuddered and asked, "Is that any improvement on a ghost?"

Stringer had brought along enough grub for himself, if he ate sparingly. Concepción had grown up eating every once in a while. So they agreed on having each other for breakfast, enjoyed one smoke and canteen water for dessert, and got up to get going again. She was still upset about the spooky lights she'd seen, or said she had. He told her his Army rifle could kill, easy, at a mile. So she calmed down when she noticed how much nothing there was all around them.

They stopped before fording Cherry Creek to drain and refill all their canteens and water bags. The streambed was wider and more braided now. But the water ran cool and clear. Stringer thought back to the last time the morning sun hadn't been this ferocious and told Concepción, "Rain on the flat plateau to the north must trickle down through cracks in the rocks a lot. I'd day the sources of this creek and the Tonto, farther over, have to be all-summer springs. This would be at best a damp dry wash by now if it depended on runoff alone."

She didn't seem interested. She said her village in the Sierra Apache was stuck with well water, deep well water, this late in the year. She said *arizona* meant little or scattered springs in the Papago lingo some of her wilder cousins still spoke, and that there wasn't even an arizona in her home canyon. One had to dig for water there, like most everywhere else in the territory.

Stringer didn't want to be ghosted from the skyline as they followed a well-mapped route alongside the only running water within miles. So they forged due east, farther, until they topped a ridge running northeast to southwest, in line with the valley whose limits were getting harder to define. Stringer saw other, higher ridges all around that would have made as good a boundry on Patty's map. The valley floor was getting ever wider as they headed southwest and the creek down the middle was starting to ox-bow as it meandered across flatter expanses. Stringer wasn't surprised to discover a narrow trail winding along the top of ridge, once they reached it. Game trails seemed to follow ridge lines as naturally as water chose the low ground between them. He swung the paint down it, enjoying their buzzard's view of the whole range below.

Concepción kept looking back as she followed aboard the old Army horse, riding astride, bareback, with her bare feet hanging wide as her knees gripped its barrel chest. It was just as well she rode Indian style, for having abandoned the old mount's saddle and bridle, Stringer had only been able to offer her an improvised length of pigging, looped over the chestnut's lower jaw behind its teeth. So far, Concepción was showing more spirit than her beat-up old mount. He could only hope she could handle it in an emergency.

He warned her to pay attention to the way they were going instead of where they'd been. She still had the half-empty pistol that had likely killed her father, and since she'd admired the Krag bayonet so much, he'd let her tuck that in her waistband, scabbard and all. But there was nothing behind them within range of knife slash or pistol ball, and the trailside shrubbery ahead was starting to get serious.

He thought about that as a stirrup-high sticker bush grabbed at a spur buckle. The slope to his right was starting to bush up as well, and the grass between was shorter, with the bare dirt exposed by sheet erosion here and there. To his left the range didn't look like range as much as it looked like plain old desert. That was likely a sign of misuse too. It was said than in the old days, when whites had first seen it, the Arizona desert had been more like semi-arid rolling prairie. But grass barely holding its own between rare rains couldn't take much grazing, and there was no sense starting a herd of cows or sheep if one didn't fancy a big one. So the beef boom of the '80s had sure scalped Arizona good, leaving tougher plants that even sheep had trouble digesting.

He spotted a clump of pioneering pear and called back, "Watch you bare feet, honey. Cactus coming up."

Concepción swung her ankle up but replied loftily, "You call this cactus? Come with me to the Sierra Apache and I will show you cactus. This salad green is nothing to what we grow south of the Salt!"

He didn't argue. She was right. Prickly pear was a pioneer species or glorified weed that grew anywhere the ground was dry at all. He'd seen it fighting ponderosa pine for room on drier slopes of his own Sierra Nevada, and some said it even grew on Cape Cod, back east. But just the same, it was an indicator of fast-draining soil. It had trouble getting started where grass roots slowed the runoff enough to matter. He glanced to his right again, and yeah, the slopes were getting thirstier and thirstier looking, with dotted lines of chaparral winding down the ever-more-frequent gullies. The ridge they were riding was now solid chaparral. He was sorry now that he hadn't thought to pick up chaps with his saddle. He glanced back and saw his part-Papago companion was coping with it all right, despite her less formal riding gear.

As he swung his eyes forward again he found himself staring an old calico longhorn in the face. The spooked-looking critter tossed its wicked horns and spun around to crash out of sight in the chaparral. Concepción laughed. Stringer said, "Easy for you to say. It would have gored my leg first if it hadn't been so polite. I think we just met part of the legendary lost herd of old Tom Graham. Have you noticed something else about this range of late?"

She said, "Si, the desert is moving back to reclaim it. I could have told you that, Stuarto. You know I rode in from the south with my poor Papacito and Ramon. It gets worse between here and the Salt. By the time Cherry Creek joins the main stream, it is only a trickle running across the desert in a deep arroyo, so it waters nothing."

He rode on, talking half to himself, as he said, "I suspect we're working our way off the range the green-light hombres seem to be managing, and I still can't figure why."

She said, "Stuarto, you are speaking silly, even though I love you. What makes you think the range to the north is being, how you say, managed? Is no-

body living there. Is no stock grazing there. Who
could be managing it, for why?"

It was a good question. He said, "I don't know
who or why yet. But I grew up on dry range that had
to be managed, so I know it when I see it. You're
right about the chaparral and worse ahead. Even had
I not just spooked wild stock, I'd suspect it was
being grazed by more than the grass can stand up to.
I reckon we're southwest of anything anyone's interested in."

She said, "I wish we'd known the abandoned
stock was down here among this chaparral instead of
up where they murdered my father and brother. But
how can you say that was managed range if the only
stock we found there had strayed over from the Tonto
Basin?"

He shrugged and said, "It works a couple of ways.
The easy way would be that they don't watch it all
the time. They just patrol it every now and again to
make sure it stays empty. Stock and wild game grazing this far down would naturally drift back up to all
that good grass and water when nobody was about.
Then it would spook back here when the gang rode
down from the north to scare and burn. That grass
upstream hadn't been grazed since the last green-up.
Yet there was no last year's thatch or serious weed
sprout. The plains Indians used to burn the prairie
clean from time to time. It makes for a thick sod of
good grazing if it's kept clear of either too much
stock or encroaching chaparral. So that's how they're
managing the upper valley, whether they know
they're doing it or not. They might be just trying to
keep it empty."

Naturally she asked why, and naturally he

couldn't tell her why. He said, "They just are. If I knew why, I'd be in a better position to guess who."

She said, "It makes no sense, Stuarto. I can see why any number of desperadoes would wish for to grab such good land. I can see why someone might wish for to hold a mining claim against all comers, even cows. There is no mining in these hills, and even if there was, what would be the sense of simply sitting on a claim and not working it?"

He said, "I just said I couldn't figure any sensible reason for what's been going on here for some time. But unless the mastermind is a rich as well as total lunatic, he has to have his reasons."

She asked why there had to be a mastermind, and he told her, "Aside from the fact someone keeps sending hired guns, not loco guns, to gun me, no one cuss would even try to hold this much open range against so many others. Whether ghost stories or something dirtier, the mastermind has been burning out and running off new settlers since the last known claimant to any part of this valley was murdered, maybe by the same rascals, a good ten years ago."

She said, "I know little of your Anglo laws. But my people say that once land has been abandoned seven years, it belongs to anyone who wants it."

He nodded and said, "Old Spanish and Old English Common Law are both based on Roman notions, and seven does seem the magic number left over from long ago. Whether either of those old feuding clans held legal or squatting title to the same range would be moot today."

She asked, "Does that mean that neither a Graham nor a Tewksbury who'd survived could return to reclaim his or her land now?"

He said, "A *he* would have more luck than a *she* at the land office. But anyone related to the old warring factions would have the same rights, no more, no less, as anyone else if they wanted to file a formal homestead claim on any part of the valley now. The homestead act only allows you a quarter section on such well-watered and flat land. But I must say that would be tempting to many a stockman I know. Most so-called ranches are just a quarter-section homespread surrounded by open range. If I was out to start a beef operation in such an out-of-the-way place, I reckon I'd claim that abandoned Tewksbury site, along with its headwater springs, and that's no doubt why it gets burnt out so regular. Someone doesn't *want* anyone living there."

She repeated that it made no sense to hog a place unless one wanted it for some sensible reason. He told her they were talking in circles and asked her to tell him more about the country ahead instead of what he'd already seen.

He was sorry he had, by the time she'd listed every abandoned 'dobe and the ghost story that went with it, all the way down the abandoned valley. So they stopped to rest their ponies and share a noonday can of tomatoes in the shade of some ridgetop boulders bridged over by wind-tortured mesquite branches.

She thought it was a neat place to get out of the sun for a spell, and he found it pretty neat to get out of his duds and back into her for a spell. But they'd just gotten their second wind and he was about to remount her when he heard the popping of chaparral not too far off and got off Concepción to grope for his jeans in a hurry. She said, "Pooh, is only more

wild cows, querido. Get back here and treat me wild
again, eh?"

He said, "Hold the fort. I told you I used to herd
cows. They don't move that serious through sticker
bush unless someone is herding them."

He saw he was right when a few moments later,
dressed and armed to receive company, he eased out
of their love nest to see four riders and perhaps a
dozen longhorns moving his way along the same
ridge. He recognized them as the Hash Knife hands
he'd met before. Montana recognized him at the
same time and called out, "Stand clear, newspaper
boy. These critters are half wild and all horn to man
on foot."

Stringer held his ground and said, "You can't
drive them through those rocks behind me."

Montana reined in, out ahead of his modest little
trail drive, and said, "Sure we can. Their horns ain't
that wide. What are you trying to hide from us
yonder, newspaper boy?"

Stringer smiled thinly and said, "That would be
my business. Just like brands of that stock you've
picked up wherever would be your business, right?"

Montana replied, "There ain't a brand on a one of
'em. I know what I said the other day about Texas
notions. But we've hunted high and low for them
eight head of Hash Knife cows, and I hate to go
home empty-handed. So just stand aside and we'll
say no more about it."

Stringer drew his six-gun and said, "I know neither of us are worth much, Montana, but it would be
a shame if the survivors had to round those cows up
all over again, and you know how gun shots spook
'em."

Montana sat his mount in thoughtful silence, staring down and hard at the gun in Stringer's hand. One of the other Hash Knife riders bulled through the chaparral to join him and ask what was up. He saw Stringer's .38, too, and said, "Oh. Well, it's for you to say, Montana."

The older hatchet-faced rider said, "I'm thinking. I'm thinking. There's four of us to one of him. On the other hand, he's got the drop and he's standing solid. He just made the interesting point that even do we win, we'll have our cows scattered by the time it's over. How do you feel about it, Pirate?"

Pirate said, "Awful. I'd hate to round 'em up all over again in this hot dry chaparral. But I don't like to look sissy neither."

Montana nodded grimly and said, "You see how it is, newspaper boy. I was brung up to act reasonable as most. But I'll be infested with ticks if I don't think you're trying to rawhide the Hash Knife for no good reason at all."

Pirate added quietly, "The Hash Knife don't rawhide easy, as many a cow thief or sheep herder meaner looking than you could tell you, if he was now in any position to talk."

Stringer tensed himself as he saw how tense this situation was getting. Then Montana laughed like hell and said, "Shoot, newspaper boy, why didn't you tell us why you didn't want us herding cows through your own private stock?"

Stringer raised a quick glance over his own shoulder to see Concepción backing his play with a scowl on her pretty face and the Krag in her hands. She might have looked more dignified, if less serious, if she'd thought to put her duds back on first.

But Montana and Pirate agreed they just weren't up to shooting it out with a naked lady, and so Montana stood in his stirrups to wave his hat and bawl to the others, "Take 'em around them rocks ahead, and don't let 'em spill down the slope on you."

Pirate ticked the brim of his own hat at Concepción with a mocking smile and spun his pony to help the other two as Montana grinned down at Stringer and said, "Don't never do that to the Hash Knife again, old son. We got us a rep to live up to."

Stringer grinned back sheepishly and said, "I just noticed as much. Before you go, one more question. Have you boys ever been rawhided by anyone else over in this valley?"

Montana shook his head and said, "That'll be the day. Even had you won, the outfit has close to a thousand guns in its payroll, and the company takes a dim view of losing either cows or cowhands. Nobody messed with the Hash Knife. That was settled back in the '80s."

Stringer nodded and said, "I heard your outfit was untouched by either the Pleasant Valley War or Geronimo. Is it safe to assume that if you wanted this abandoned range, you'd take it?"

Montana nodded and said, "Sure we would. Who could stop us? But like I said, our homespread is too far off. We're fixing to play hell getting this stock all the way home with us. But we got to. So adios, newspaper boy. You, too, señorita."

Then he rode off, laughing. Stringer was sort of sorry to see Montana and the others go. He had them figured now as what they said they were. Four honest young cowboys, armed and willing to stand up and be counted. Everyone else he'd run into down this

STRINGER ON DEAD MAN'S RANGE   117

way, save for crazy little Concepción, seemed to be a
sneaky son of a bitch who wouldn't look him in the
eye.

Nothing half as interesting happened as they rode
along the same ridge trail until sundown. Concepción
kept looking back and muttering darkly about whatever her half-Papago eyes thought they were glimps-
ing in the shimmering heat waves above the
now-solid chaparral. To calm her down he gave her
some of his own .38 rounds for her nickel-plated and
beat-up S&W and told her they seemed to be off the
disputed range now, if they were in Pleasant Valley at
all.

The map didn't say. Wherever they were wasn't
so pleasant. The ridge trail they were on was now out
of sight of Cherry Creek to their right. The valley, if
one still wanted to call it that, had widened out to a
vast flat covered with blue-gray desert scrub, and the
creek, wherever it was, had dug itself a deep ditch
winding through no longer semiarid but seriously-
arid desert. He was sure he'd ridden through and
beyond the mystery of Pleasant Valley. But this was
no place to leave a lady, and he'd wired his home
office he was headed for Globe, on the far side of the
Salt, in any case.

They both knew the coming night figured to be
their last alone together. So by tacit consent they
reined in and dismounted as the last light of gloaming showed them a swell place to bed down.

Drifting sand had settled in a smooth gentle slope
against an outcrop of pillow-shaped bedrocks, so
they wouldn't have to clear brush or worry about the
snakes of a desert evening among the same. They

could hear desert diamondbacks, or critters running from them, in the chaparral all around the natural clearing as Concepción spread their bedding while he tended to the ponies. He tethered them to mesquite they could nibble, rubbed them down, and gave them more oats than usual after watering them. His feed sack was about empty now. But they were almost back to civilization, and even the old Army stray had earned a square meal for a change.

He rejoined Concepción. She was holding his can of coffee wistfully, bayonet in the other hand, waiting for him to say. He said, "The can's already open, honey. I reckon it would be safe to build a fire tonight. We're ridden way beyond any fool secret those fools could be guarding back there. I sure wish I knew what it was. But I don't. So I'd best gather some firewood."

He did. It was easy, with half the local vegetation dead and sun-baked brittle enough to bust up with bare hands. They made a hollow in the sand, downslope from their bedding, and he got it going on the second match with only a fistful of dry-leaf kindling. Concepción had already filled the pot with canteen water. As she put it on to boil she said, "I shall brew out last coffee strong. So we won't get sleepy until you have utterly ravaged me beyond recovery. I do not wish you to forget me soon, querido. I know I shall never forget you. You were my first Anglo lover. Had I known sooner how good your people made love, I would not have waited so long."

He laughed, perhaps a little louder than he felt like laughing. He was glad she was being a good sport about it. A lot of gals tended not to be. He was feeling a mite wisful, knowing he'd no doubt miss old Concepción some future night when the moon caught him all alone in his bedroll, or with someone not as sweet and athletic. He knew she expected him to say something mushy. So he said, "I do wish things could be different, honey. But I told you my job just won't let me stay in one place long."

She said, "Si, and even if it did, I'd still be Mex, no?"

He said, "No. That's not it. I know your folk and mine have had some differences in the past. But I grew up with Mex neighbors, and one of my best boyhood chums—a kid named Pedro—got killed in the war with Spain as patriotic as the rest of us. We called him Pete. I learned a lot of Spanish from him."

She said, "I'll bet you screwed his sister, too, eh?"

He told her not to talk dirty. He had, in fact, made out sort of friendly with old Pete's kid sister that time. But she'd been sort of blond, and he'd never called her a greaser. He said, "That brush sure burns better than it makes coals. I'd better go gather some more."

He did. It didn't take long to gather an armful, if a man could stand the noise. He carried it back to the fire. Concepción wasn't there. He figured she'd gone off to enjoy a squat in private. He hunkered down to put a few more sticks on the cook fire. He heard the snick of a gun being cocked behind him and stiffened silently.

His own sidearm was still on his hip. Both the Krag and the nickle-plated S&W Concepción had found lay nearby on her blanket. But not nearby enough. So he wasn't too surprised when a male voice told him calmly, "Unbuckle that gun rig and let it fall where it may, MacKail."

He did what he was ordered to do. He had no other choice. As he squatted there, six-gun on the sand beside him, his unknown tormentor said, "Stand up and turn around now, slow."

Stringer did so. He felt as foolish as he felt afraid when he saw who had the drop on him. The total stranger was a little bearded gent with a battered desert-rat look to him and a single-action Colt '74. But the old thumb-buster was cocked as well as trained on him. So all Stringer could do about it was nod and mutter, "Howdy. Since you know me by name, it's safe to assume you're interested in something more than coffee, right?"

The older man nodded and said, "I am. Have you any last words for me to carry back to the boss?"

Stringer said, "I might. It depends on who your boss might be, and what in thunder he might want."

The man who had the drop on him said, "I'll ask all the questions here. You'll answer 'em, if you don't cotton to the notion of dying slow, gut shot."

Stringer said, "I don't reckon I'd enjoy that. But since you mean to kill me in any case, I see no harm in laying all the cards face up on the table."

Before the other man could argue, Stringer quickly pointed out, "I don't know what it is that your boss is afraid I'll find out. As you can see from this fool fire, I rode all the way through the range you boys are haunting without seeing a thing worth printing in the *San Francisco Sun*. Can't you even give me a hint?"

The older man shook his head and said, "Not hardly. The boss pays me to protect his secrets, not blabber about 'em. So what do you think the secret might be, MacKail?"

Stringer said, "I told you I was stumped. It has to be mighty important, unless you're determined past common sense. Can I assume you're either a Graham or a Tewksbury? No offense, but you look old enough to have rid in their war a few years back."

As his newspaper experience had led him to hope, the old gunslick was as interested in hearing the opinions of others about himself as most folk were. He said, "Guess again. You might say I'm imported as experienced outside help. Who I might be working for is less important than who you might think I'd be working for. So it's your turn."

Stringer shrugged and said, "I could give it to you numerical or alphabetical if I possessed a county register, and I can't say for sure we're talking about Navajo County. Don't it end at about the Mogollon Rim?"

The old man chuckled and said, "You don't know nothing. It's sort of a shame, seeing as I got to kill you anyways, old son."

He raised the gun in his hand to do so. Then the muzzle gave a sudden jerk and fired well over Stringer's head as Stringer dropped to claw his own gun from its holster in the sand.

But as he rolled over once for luck and came up in a fighting crouch, he saw the murderous old man was already hitting the ground, face down, with the brass-bound hilt of a Krag sword bayonet sticking straight up from between his shoulder blades.

As Stringer pondered this, Concepción stepped into view from behind the just-visible rocks she'd made her throw from. She wore a little Mona Lisa on her half-Indian face as she stared down at victim, saying, "That blade has a nice balance. I as afraid the range was a little far."

Stringer whistled softly and said, "I can see why the Apache felt it best not to mess with Papago. It's sure lucky you felt the call of nature well before he moved in on our fire light."

She asked, "What call of nature? I heard the fool coming long before he got here. He didn't dismount before he was maybe fifty yards out, over that way. I told you I thought someone was still following us, Sturato."

He nodded and said, "I never argue with Indian blood about such notions, honey. We'd best let the fire go out. I'm pretty sure he rode on after us alone, maybe in hopes of a bonus, but I've had enough dismal surprises for one night."

Concepción bent over, picked up the rifle, and said, "You go gather in his horse. I'll climb up on the rocks and make sure we're alone while our coffee boils. I told you why I wanted to fill both our bellies with good strong coffee tonight, and I meant it."

He didn't argue. He went out to find the dead man's pony. It was a bay mare, and the other mounts seemed glad to meet it. He unsaddled it, watered it, fed it, and then dragged the old man farther out on the desert flat by his boot heels, making another twenty-odd dollars and no further information on the deal.

By the time he got back the fire was out and Concepción was undressed. They drank every bit of the black coffee she'd made first, and she still damn near screwed him unconcious.

CHAPTER
EIGHT

It was too blamed hot to more than kiss when they finally reached the shallow Salt River the next afternoon. Concepción seemed so pleased by that surplus sword bayonet, that he let her keep it, along with the dead man's saddled pony and the old Army mount. He offered her half the money he'd found in the pockets of two dead rascals. She protested that she couldn't take dinero from a man she'd made love to, lest he think her a mere *puta*. He told her to consider it a reward for saving his life. She settled for all the metal coinage, including one ten-dollar gold piece, saying nobody where she hailed from accepted paper money in any case, and that the two ponies alone would do her proud in her home village. But when he leaned out to kiss her again she looked away and murmured, "Go with God, Stuarto. I do not wish for you to remember me with tears in my eyes." So he nodded, swung his buckskin around, and loped off, not looking back.

He forded the Salt a mile or so up and found a

well-traveled wagon trace that had to lead to Globe, since there was nothing much else within miles. He rested and swapped mounts a time or two and got into town just before sundown.

Globe, Arizona Territory, was most famous for having been the first place a wild west show was called a rodeo, and having been at least close to the last recorded stagecoach holdup in these United States. Globe was also the seat of Gila County. After that it didn't have much to say for itself.

The population hovered around five thousand, depending on whether the herd was in town or not. The town fed boiler water to a Southern Pacific spur line really more interested in some nearby copper mines, and in return got to ship out beef from surrounding spreads. There was talk about a big irrigation project any day now. But so far that day had yet to dawn, so Globe mostly dozed in the heat of day and raised a little hell at night.

Not too much hell. A lot of Globe was run by Mormons, who didn't even hold with tea or coffee. The Mexican and Texican element naturally tended to drink more seriously. But between roundups the hard drinkers tended to be broke.

Stringer stabled his mounts with a livery hand who acted reasonably sober, and got directions to the local Western Union office. There he discovered a wire from old Sam Barca waiting for him, and reading it, he was made to feel sort of dumb.

For without leaving his glass-walled box in Frisco, old Sam had tracked down all sorts of gents by wiring other newspaper men back and forth. Sam wanted to know why on earth he'd ever headed for Globe, if that was where he was right now.

Sam said he'd located Commodore Perry Owens in Seligman, one hell of a ways off, where the Chino crossed the Santa Fe. He added the *Sun* wouldn't pay Stringer's expenses to Seligman, since the ex-sheriff had already granted an interview by wire that they couldn't print.

Old Owens had cussed the brains of the voters more than he'd cussed the vote count. He was currently running a saloon in Seligman, and since he didn't dispute the election results in anything more sensible than Anglo-Saxon verbs one couldn't even repeat in mixed company, the editorial staff of the *Sun* was satisfied the election had been an honest fluke. However, in view of the language, Western Union reduced to "blank, blank, blank sons of blank blank blanks," the charge he was given to strong drink these days could have been the reason they'd voted him out. Barca said he was sorry he'd sent Stringer on a snipe hunt, said the *Sun* would still pay for half of it, and ordered him to come on home.

Stringer started to wire back. But he knew he'd just get hell, and wind up paying for it out of his own pocket. So he crumpled Sam's night letter and tossed it in the wastebasket.

Outside an old Mex with a pole wick was lighting a streetlamp as the Arizona sky above started to go from tangerine to lilac. But there was still enough gloaming to see by as Stringer heard a rumble and a roar and turned to see a big ore wagon, drawn by a six-mule team, proceeding in his direction down the center of the street at considerable speed.

A boy of no more than six or seven was alone on the driver's plank, hauling back on the reins as hard as a little kid could, with one bitty foot braced against the brake pole to no avail.

There were several ways a man might try to stop a runaway ore wagon. The heroic way would be to dash out and try to grab the lead mule's bridle, and likely get trampled to death before the wheels could finish him off. Stringer chose a smarter way. He started running the same way until the whole shebang passed him. Then he swung in, sprinted harder, and hauled himself over the tailgate.

The kid was bawling a blue streak as Stringer crawled over the jagged copper ore to join him. Some of the things the kid was calling the mules sounded even dirtier, coming from such a little shaver. Stringer took the reins from him, braced a bigger booted instep against the brake pole, and wound up teaching the kid some additional mule-skinner words before the infernal team got tired of dragging a loaded wagon with its wheels locked, and gave up, panting and cussing back in mule.

Stringer hadn't been the only one in town chasing the runaway wagon. He'd just run better. A lady in a mother-hubbard and sunbonnet had the rest of the crowd beat by a fine lead. She rushed to identify the wayward child as "Willy, you'll be the death of me!" before she hauled him off the rig by his belt, got a good grip on one ear, and smacked him good with her free hand. A gent wearing laced boots and a red face panted to a wobble-kneed halt beside him and gasped, "Hit him again, ma'am. That's my load he just drove off with!"

But as others joined them, most agreeing the little rascal deserved to be horse-whipped if not lynched, the young mother was bawling as loud as her Willy as she hugged him and shook him and asked if he thought he'd live after all.

Stringer saw the mining man had commenced to treat his lead mule like a long lost child too. So he wrapped the reins around the brake pole and dropped to the dusty street. The gal blubbering all over her fool kid wasn't the first in the crowd to call Stringer a hero. But she must have been listening, for she let go everything but Willy the Death's right ear and dragged him over so she could hug Stringer too. She hugged sisterly, but he could still tell she wasn't wearing any whalebone under that thin, loose summer print. She said he'd saved her only child, which didn't surprise him much, and added she was in his debt and didn't know how she'd ever pay him. She was pretty under her sunbonnet, but she didn't look like that kind of a gal. So he said, "It was on the house, ma'am. I needed the exercise. Nobody was hurt. So all I want is a word with your Willy the Death here."

She stood the red-faced and tear-streaked kid to attention by his ear and told him to listen to the gentleman, sharp.

Stringer told the kid, "I used to wonder what it would be like to drive a mule team, too, Willy. I was older than you when they let me, and the results were much the same. So I want your word, man to man, you won't ever try that again until you've got at least a hundred fifty pounds of body weight and a twelve-foot whip on your side."

The kid answered with a wretched sob. His mother hit him again and told him to speak up. Stringer said, "I reckon he answered me right, ma'am. I know *I* would, were I in his shoes."

The original owner of the team and rig rejoined them to say, "Well, no real damage done. So I'll settled for ten bucks, ma'am."

Before she could answer, Stringer growled, "No you won't. You was as much at fault as the boy here."

The mule skinner scowled and said, "Not hardly, stranger. That ornery little cuss had no business crawling up on my wagon and driving off with it."

Stringer said, "He didn't drive off with it. He didn't get the chance. Your mules bolted, as mules will, the moment they sensed a weak grip and no brakes."

The shorter but stockier man growled, "But that as it may, I never gave anyone but me permission to go anywhere near my mules or my customer's ore."

Stringer said, "How could you if you wasn't watching? Since said ore had to come from the mountains to the west, and since the railroad spur is farther down the street, not where you had all that ore parked, it's safe to assume you parked it there to enter some saloon or worse, right?"

The outraged property owner looked away, but growled, "Where a man might refresh hisself after a long haul down from the Sierra Apache is his own durn business, ain't it?"

Stringer shook his head and said, "Not if you want to take this lady and her boy to law. That's the only way you'll ever get one dollar off her, and of course the court records will have to show exactly where you might have been at the time this bitty boy proved boys will be boys."

"What are you, a lawyer?"

"Nope. I can't charge for legal advice. But I'm

telling you free that you're as much in the wrong as the boy here, and that if I *was* a lawyer I'd advise *her* to sue *you* for nearly killing her child with an attractive nuisance. That's what the law calls it when a fool leaves anything dangerous that might attract kids unguarded, which is what you done, as any fool can plainly see."

There was a murmur of agreement from the others all around. The mule skinner said, "Oh, let's not get all het up about nothing. Like I said, no harm's been done."

Stringer took the young mother's arm and murmured, "Let's get you and Willy the Death back on the walk before he can change his mind again, ma'am."

She didn't argue. She just dragged her fool kid after them by the ear until they were well clear of the crowd. Once he had them on the walk, Stringer let go her arm, ticked his hat brim to her and said, "It was nice meeting up with you folk. But I'm stuck here in Globe at least overnight, and I got to scout up a place to bed down now."

She brightened and said, "Then I *can* repay you after all. For I am Prue Reynolds, and I run one of the most respectable boarding houses in Globe!"

Then she glanced down at the shirt he was wearing under his denim jacket and added uncertainly, "Oh, dear, how awkward. You don't seem to be a saint."

He smiled uncertainly and replied, "No, ma'am. Just a hero. I doubt I'll ever make saint."

She laughed and explained, "I meant latter day saint, or Morman, as the vulgar put it. You have a tobacco tag hanging out of your shirt pocket."

He nodded and said, "Bull Durham. Red Robin smells even worse. I plead guilty to coffee and even tea, Miss Prue, so let's say no more about it. I wouldn't want to upset your other boarders."

She took his arm back and insisted, "Don't be silly. I've taken in gentiles before. It's you who might find my house rules a mite bothersome. But you won't be able to beat my price, in Globe or anywhere else, for I'll not take a cent from a man who is a hero, however he may mock himself, and we eat the same or better than anyone else, if you can survive apple pie without tea or coffee."

He said he was willing to try if he could smoke later, out on the steps. She said that sounded fair. So he went with her. His luggage was in the tack room at the livery. But he didn't think an overnight stay would be worth the fuss.

They led him up a narrower side street that was trying to be tree lined. All the cottonwoods some optimist had planted a spell back were dead. But when they got to her picket fence, he saw a dusty but living rambler rose crawling along it, and the dooryard had been planted with sunflowers, Mexican poppies, and other stuff that could stand up to the Arizona sun as long as it got plenty of water.

Inside they found the parlor filled with other boarders who were barely managing to keep from cussing about supper being so late that evening. The Mormon-hired girls had refused to dish it out until their boss lady got back with Willy the Death, wherever he'd run off to this time.

Prue Reynolds apologized, told her hired gals not to do that no more, and sent Willy the Death off to bed with no supper before she introduced Stringer to her other guests. He noticed that while she told them what a hero he was, and most seemed to agree, she neglected to mention he was gentile as they all went into the dining room to squat and grub.

He managed to get the Bull Durham tag out of sight as he hung his hat and gun up by the dining room door. It was easy enough to just bow his head and grit his teeth as their pretty hostess said grace at the head of the table. The Book of Mormon wasn't exactly the Good Book Stringer had been brought up on. But as he took both with a grain of salt, he didn't notice any great difference between her simple prayer and all the others he'd had to sit through, feeling more hungry than religious.

The others must have been hungry, too, judging from the way they dug in to her fine feed. One old gent, who dressed like a parson and looked even snootier, grabbed far and wide for bread and butter, as if he feared an impending famine. A mousy little gal sitting next to him in widow's weeds kept giving him dirty looks. Stringer didn't blame her. The hired gals kept bringing more bread from the kitchen as if they had a bakery going back there. Stringer concentrated more on the roast beef and mashed spuds, both swimming in mighty fine gravy. He even found the butter beans served with the more manly food enjoyable, after a long hard ride on short rations. Prue pressed second helpings on everyone. Only the old parsony cuss ate a third. Then they brought apple pie out, each heroic slice served with a wedge of orange cheese, and Stringer forgave their church its ban on coffee when he saw he got to wash the pie down with mighty fine lemonade. They hadn't stinted on the lemons, and there were still chunks of ice floating in the pitchers the help placed at each end of the table. He was glad the pretty young landlady could afford such fine accommodations. He was glad he wasn't paying for it too. From the way the others dressed, and from all but that one old slob's table manners, they were prosperous ladies and gents. He noticed that saints didn't seem to hold with the usual custom of chasing the ladies from the table after dessert so the gents could talk more dirty over brandy and cigars. That was likely because their church forbade either brandy or cigars. It must have forbade dirty stories as well, for the four or five gals around the table stayed put and joined in the conversation, which seemed to be mostly about water.

The old parsony gent, who seemed to get on with the others well enough when he wasn't snatching food from their plates, did most of the talking as he held forth on the awful way the gentiles in Washington were running Arizona Territory. Stringer knew enough about the Mormon Corridor or Mormon Delta up Utah way to follow some of his drift. He said his and other Morman families had made the desert blossom as the rose up north by honest toil and common sense. He said, "None of this rain-poor land out here can prosper without irrigation. We'd have starved to death on the shores of the great salt lake if we'd tried to get by as these ninnies down this way do. Think of the truck crops this valley could ship, if only the gentiles would work together instead of fighting one another over marginal and wide-scattered grazing land."

A slightly younger but wiser-looking Morman in a business suit shot a thoughtful look at Stringer's riding outfit and said, "Raising stock is the easy way to start, T.S. It takes a lot of money as well as hard work to irrigate desert land, you know."

Old T.S. struck a proud pose in his chair and said, "We had no money when we came over the south pass with Brother Brigham to the place of revelation. It was desert as dry as any down here. The mountain men warned us corn wouldn't grow in the Great Basin, and they were right, until we changed it to a new Garden of Eden by damming and ditching the water that had up until then been wasted on the parched salt flats to the west. We'd have starved had we tried to get by as stock men that far from any market, on such marginal range land. But by the time the Great California Rush was on, we were in a position to sell fresh produce to the passing wagon trains at a profit!"

Stringer knew that was true. His grandfather, who'd been a '49er, had often cussed about the price set on cabbages and turnips along that stretch of the trail. But he didn't think he ought to bring that up at this late date.

The more thoughtful Mormon businessman said, "That was then and this is now, T.S. Our elders moved west to Deseret simply because in those days it wasn't under U.S. jurisdiction. They didn't need money to tame the desert, and while they were at it, the Utes. They were free to experiment. They were free to change the courses of rivers with nobody upstream but a fool Indian to argue about it. This is the twentieth century, and Arizona was never Utah to begin with. A settler now can't just go out and dam any old dry wash he wants to. He needs a lawyer as much or more than he needs a shovel. The homestead act only gives one free claim to a quarter section. You have to buy all the other land you'd need for even a modest irrigation project. And no doubt some Indian or Mex would run to the federal government, complaining you'd violated his water rights, before you could even get started."

He sipped more lemonade and added, "Mark my words. It's going to take the federal government itself to irrigate this part of the southwest right. Only big federal projects, agreed on by all the voters, could untangle all the conflicting interests in these parts. We'll probably never see that in our time."

Stringer shot the younger man a thoughtful look and said, "I just came down here through some disputed range and maybe water rights, sir. Since you seem to know more about such matters than me, I'd like your opinion on a notion that just struck me."

The older man said to call him R.J. and shoot. So Stringer told them all some of his recent adventures, leaving out murder and other misbehavior the Book of Mormon might not approve, of course.

When he'd finished, the mousy little gal across from him was staring owl-eyed at him, as if she thought he might be getting set to rope the lemonade pitcher between them. Parsony old T.S. snorted in disgust and said, "I remember that range war. Like I said, gentiles don't know how to manage semidesert land. They might have made that valley blossom as the rose. But instead they ruined it by running stock on range that doesn't get twelve inches of rain a year. Then they fought like animals over the scraps left."

Stringer said, "The grass is coming back good up near the headwaters. The last I saw of Cherry Creek, it was still running between rains. I just wonder who might own all that water in a thirsty land now."

The more thoughtful R.J. said, "I can answer that. Uncle Sam. All abandoned homestead claims revert to the federal land office, and they say even the Indians avoid that old battleground now. You know how Indians feel about bloody ground, and in its day that valley got to bleed some."

The mousy little gal across the table said flatly, "It's haunted."

There was an awkward silence. Then parsony old T.S. cleared his throat and said, "The Book doesn't hold with such talk, Sister Bertha."

She sniffed defensively and said, "I know what I saw with my own eyes one night. If Brother Joseph Smith could see an angel under an apple tree in New York State, I guess I have a right to say what I saw one night up in that awful valley."

Stringer nodded at her and said, "I've never seen either an angel nor a haunt, Miss Bertha. But I'm listening with an open mind. When and where did you see whatever?"

She stared down at her lemonade glass, blushing, and almost whispered as she told him, "Five or six years back, when my late husband and me came down from Utah, looking for new lands to settle. My husband Seth had heard about the good grass and water up to Pleasant Valley. We drove up there, liked what we saw, and filed on a quarter section. Seth thought we might use the foundations and still-standing chimney of an old ruin we found near the springs that water the valley. But we were still living in our covered wagon when the haunting started."

At the head of the table Prue noticed how uneasy the mousy little gal was making almost everyone but Stringer. So she said, "We know you and Brother

Seth never proved that claim before he was taken from you, dear heart. But surely what you mean to say is that you were run back to Globe by ruffians, perhaps cowboys from the Tonto Basin, rather than, ah, superstition."

The mousy little gal shook her head stubbornly and said, "I know what I saw. We got along all right with the few cowboys who passed by from time to time. They were looking for strays, not trouble, and my Seth was a man's man who got on well with even gentiles. *He* thought I was making it up, too, until one night he saw them too. That's when we moved back to Globe to find some other way to make a living. He said our claim was all right, but not worth fighting men, let alone haunts, over."

Another lady got up and left the room with a snooty sniff. But the others stayed, no doubt as curious as Stringer was when he asked her to describe her haunts.

She looked as if she was sorry she'd started the whole deal as she said defensively, "They were sort of shiny and sort of green, like big old fireflies drifting back and forth all around us in the dark. Only they were way too big, and moved way too slow to be fireflies."

Stringer asked how she felt about railroad lanterns. She shook her head and said, "Not that green and not that bright. They were a pale, pale green, just bright enough to see against the blackness they were sort of floating through. My Seth took a shot at one. He was a sensible man, not a coward. But it just laughed at us and floated off a spell. Then, later, it came back to just float there, like it was trying to tell us something."

Stringer nodded and said, "Others would seem to have gotten the same message. You say you *heard* as well as saw that spook light?"

She said, "It's true. It's really true, no matter what you all think. It laughed crazy and mean. It didn't sound human, but it didn't sound like a critter neither. Oh, I forgot. The night we decided to give up, we heard wolves ahowling all about too."

R.J. said gently, "There are no wolves in these parts, Sister Bertha."

And she said, "That's what Seth said. He said lobo wolves belonged over in Apache country, not on abandoned range where there was nothing for 'em to feed on, save for us. So in the morning we packed up and lit out. We never regretted it. Seth found a decent job down this way and kept it, untroubled by haunts, until that mine cave-in last year."

Then she leaped up to run out of the room with her hands to her little red face.

In the awkward silence that followed, other's excused themselves from the table as well. Stringer didn't know what to do until Prue Reynolds told him she'd show him to his room now, if he'd like to see it.

She did and he did. It was a sweet-smelling corner room with cross ventilation. She showed him the washstand in the corner and hinted she had indoor plumbing down at the end of the hall if he required, eh, anything else.

He said he wasn't sleepy, and asked if he could smoke out front. She said he could. So they parted friendly at the head of the stairs and he went down them.

He'd been sitting there about ten minutes, surprised at how good tobacco could taste when one thought of it as forbidden fruit rather than something to do with one's hands, when the garden gate swung open and a tall gent in a black suit came over to ask where he might find one Stringer MacKail.

Stringer, had, of course, taken his hat and gun rig out front with him. So he just rose to even the odds as he said, "You've found him. What's your pleasure?"

The stranger opened the front of his frock coat to flash silver in the moonlight and say, "I'm Ed Nolan. Deputy Ed Nolan. We just got an odd wire from Saint John's that you might be able to help us out with. Is it true you just rode down through Pleasant Valley?"

Stringer sat back down, saying, "I did. Can't say I know Saint John's that well. I left from Holbrook."

Nolan put one boot up on a step to relax it as he nodded and said, "Not many have. Saint John's got aced out when the Santa Fe chose to run its tracks through Holbrook years ago. Anyhow, there's a gent in Saint Johns named Barth, Sol Barth, I think. He's said to be one of the bigger frogs in that little puddle. He says he's missing some riders. One's named Gus Warner, and he's described as an old geezer a mite long in the tooth but a hard worker. The other would be Hamp Coleman, younger than Warner but older than you or me. We was wondering if you might have encountered either in your recent travels."

Stringer was pretty sure he had. On the other hand he wasn't dead certain, and explaining dead men could be a bother when one didn't have to. So he said, "I ran into some riders off the Hash Knife. One was called Montana and another was Pirate. Can't say what the other two might have answered to. Oh, yeah, I met a stray Army mount up that way too. We parted company at the Salt. Can't say where he drifted after that."

Nolan said, "Now that's sure odd. Barth wired that his man, Warner, was last seen riding a pony with a remount brand. Don't ask me why. The Army sells 'em off when the oats and Indians are down. You say Warner's mount was just wandering about on its own up yonder?"

Stringer nodded and said, "It was running loose with neither saddle nor bridle the first time I saw it in Pleasant Valley." Which was the simple truth when one thought about it, word for word.

Nolan said, "Well, they do tell funny stories about that old abandoned range. Would it be too much to ask why you decided to haunt it some as well?"

Stringer said, "I've nothing to hide about my reasons for wanting a look-see. I'm a newspaper man. I thought there could be a story. I'm still trying to figure one out. Having just passed through from one end to the other, it is my considered opinion that there's nobody living up there now. You've heard the tales about haunts chasing new settlers out, of course?"

Nolan nodded and said, "I have. Did you see any spooks up that way, MacKail?"

Stringer said, "Not personal. What were those other riders doing on the same range, if I may ask?"

Nolan shrugged and said, "Their boss didn't say. He didn't even tell us what they did for him, let alone why they'd want to be doing it so far from Saint John's. He just asked us to see if we could find out whatever happened to 'em."

"That sounds like a boss who worries about his help. But how come you came looking for me, of all people? I've never heard of any gent called Sol Barth."

Nolan said, "Neither had I until I asked around town. Some old-timers recall Barth as a merchant and horse trader with a Mexican wife of good family and a finger in many a pie. He must know more about you. He mentioned you by name and suggested you might know something about his missing help. Before you ask how I tracked *you* down, don't never stop a runaway team on Main Street if you don't aim to be well-knowed in a town this size."

Stringer smiled and said he'd keep that in mind. Then he said, "You can tell Sol Barth for me that I have never been formally introduced to anyone called Gus Warner or Hamp Coleman, but that I may pay a social call on him if ever I'm up his way."

Nolan said, "I ain't about to waste money on wires that don't say more than that. If his boys are gone, they're gone, until someone tells me where in thunder they may be. Before *you* turn up missing, MacKail, would it be too much to ask where you may be headed next?"

Stringer sighed and said, "No place, until I rest up some. Then my boss wants me to come on home to Frisco."

Nolan nodded and said, "If you take the spur down to the main S.P. line, it ain't too long a trip by rail."

Stringer said, "I've been studying on that. The Santa Fe runs the same way, and I hate to be called a horse thief. I'm stuck with a pair of livery mounts from Holbrook. So I reckon I'll catch a westbound from there."

Nolan frowned down at him and said, "I'd have thought you'd seen enough of Pleasant Valley and all the desert north and south of the same by now, MacKail."

Stringer said, "I have indeed, and it was tedious the first time. But now that I know the way and how much grub to take, I ought to make better time going back."

Nolan stood in silent thought for a time before he said, "I hope you won't take this unfriendly. But I am getting the distinct impression someone is bullshitting me. What's all this high-summer riding through nothing much really about, MacKail?"

Stringer said, "I wish I knew. It wasn't my idea to begin with. I wanted to publish a story about the Frisco Chinatown. My boss sensed a good feature on Sheriff Commodore Perry Ownes and the old range wars he was involved in. Only Owens is now running a saloon in Seligman, and everyone else involved seems to be dead or scattered. As to ghost stories, they're only worth writing when you have a good ending, and I can't even come up with a sensible beginning. My paper's not about to run a mess of vague rumors about mysterious boomps in the night. So unless I meet a ghost personal going back the other way, I reckon I'll have wasted a lot of time admiring mighty empty scenery."

Nolan said, "I'd offer you an armed escort if we had more'n haunt tales to go on. It's your funeral if you're holding out on us."

Stringer said he'd keep that in mind, and Nolan left. Stringer field-stripped his spent smoke lest he shock anyone tending a Mormon garden, and got up to turn in. The house was quiet as he eased up the dimly lit stairs. His room was pitch-black. He lit a match to get his bearings, and let it go out once he had the simple layout figured. He tried to lock the door. There was no key on either side of the spring latch. He frowned and slid a chair over to the door. Its back wasn't tall enough to lock under the knob, but at least it would slide noisy on the hardwood floor if anyone got sneaky.

Having done all he could, he hung his gun handy on the bedpost farthest from the door, undressed, and gave himself a bath at the washstand in the dark. Then he slipped between the clean, crisp lavender-scented sheets and fell right off, as the past few nights of sleeping on hard ground caught up with him.

But, as ever, Stringer tended to sleep light in a strange bed, even with the door locked. So when the door opened to slide chair legs loud as hell, Stringer was sitting up with his .38 trained before the dark figure outlined by the hall light could get it shut again.

As the room was once more plunged in blackness, Stringer rolled off the far side of the bed, gun still trained, and told his unseen visitor, "I got five in the wheel, all for you, if you don't say something friendly fast."

He heard someone whisper, "Where are you? I can't see you."

He said, "That makes two of us, ma'am. Let's keep it like that until you tell me what this is all about."

She whispered, "Not so loud! I didn't mean to

startle you. I ducked in here because I had to. That nosy old T.S. is just down the hall in the bathroom. I didn't want him to see me sneaking back to my own room next to the bath."

Stringer asked, "From where?"

She replied, "I just left a sandwich and a glass of milk in little Willy's room. I know what a scamp he is, but I fear I'm just not as strict as common sense says we should be when I think of hungry children."

He had her figured out now. He got back in bed to reholster his gun as he said, "Your secret is safe with me, ma'am. I had a strict mother one time."

She said, "Not so loud, I pray you. I don't want the others to know, and that horrid old man down the hall gossips like an old biddy hen. I wish he'd go back to bed. But once he's in there, he's likely to stay half the night. I think he reads on the . . . never mind. I hope I'm not making you uncomfortable?"

As a matter of fact she was, but it wasn't polite to mention erections to a lady who hesitated to say crapper. So he told her it was jake with him if she wanted to stay a spell.

He hadn't meant that as seriously as she took it. But when she said, "My, it's cold in here with all the windows open," and got in bed with him, he'd have felt even sillier doing anything else. But as he took her in his arms, she stiffened and said, "Heavens! You're not wearing your nightgown!"

He said, "I don't own one, and you're sort of overdressed for occasions like this. So why don't we just get all this infernal flannel out of the way?"

She gasped and asked what he thought he was doing as she pulled her nightgown down as fast as he could pull it up. He kissed her to keep her from asking such dumb questions. But though she kissed back more sweetly than passionate, and continued to resist his free hand, he gave up and told her, "I'm sorry if I misjudged your odd views on avoiding the cold desert night air. I might enjoy kid games more if I was a kid. But whatever in thunder you think you're doing, it strikes me as cruelty to animals. So why don't you just get out of my fool bed and we'll say no more about it."

She snuggled closer and said, "I can't leave until the hallway is clear, and it feels so cozy under the covers with you like this."

He said, "That does it. Unless we assume Willy the Death was a product of immaculate conception, this conversation is getting dumb as hell. So get up or let's get to acting grown-up. There are limits to my genteel upbringing, ma'am."

She asked, "Why are you fussing at me? Have I done something wrong?"

He said, "Not yet," and kissed her again, harder, as he rolled atop her, jerked the hem of her flannel nightgown just high enough to matter, and got in her awkwardly, but mighty fine.

As she felt his turgid shaft inside her she gasped, "Oh, no, not that!" then wrapped her legs around his waist to pull him deeper, sobbing, "Oh, Lord, please don't let that horrid old T.S. find out about this."

He kissed her ear and whispered, "Nobody will, if you'll just hold it down to a roar, honey. I was hoping like hell you meant it like this when you said you felt eternal to me. But to tell the truth, I thought you was too prim and proper."

She moaned, "I try to be. But a woman has needs and—oh, sweet chariot, come any time you want!"

He did. He could tell she'd enjoyed it as much or more. From the way she'd damned near raped him, coy as she'd talked her way into bed with him, he suspected it had been some time since she'd been with a man. They'd never gotten around to just who Willy the Death's father might have been. He obviously wasn't around at the moment.

As they lay entwined, getting used to each other's flesh now that the ice had been broken, he started inching her nightgown out of the way some more. She murmured, "Oh, no, I couldn't. I was raised to be modest, and not even my late husband ever saw me stark."

He kissed her again and soothed, "That's all right. I can't see a thing, and you don't know what you've been missing if you've never done it naked before."

He was right. She protested feebly until her naked nipples were pressed to his bare chest. Then she gasped, "Oh, my, that does feel lovely!" and helped him get the last of the dumb, thick flannel off over her head. But as she took him in her now bare arms and held him close to her soft warm body, he began to wonder how anyone built like this could look like she did in her thin mother-hubbard. Such shapeless outfits could, it was all too true, hide a multitude of sins. But there wasn't anything *wrong* with the shapely torso he was enjoying, it was just plain different. As he moved his hips to pleasure her, he explored the rest of her with his hands, and while she said she loved that, too, it was becoming increasingly clear he was not making love to Prue Reynolds.

There was no polite way at this late date to ask a lady who on earth one was laying. He'd just have to wait until they got to stop a while. Then he could use a relaxing smoke as an excuse to strike a match and see who she might be.

Meanwhile, whoever the hell she was had gotten over her shy act, and it was amusing to consider what she'd looked like in the past, doing it on top, if she'd never done it with her nightgown off before. As she bounced above him skillfully, he decided that was likely another attempt at delicacy rather than the whole truth. He'd spent a lot more time getting this far with gals who started out talking sassy and even smoking in public.

After she'd climaxed thrice, or said she had, and begged for mercy until she got her breath back, Stringer dismounted and rolled his bare feet to the floor on the far side to grope for his shirt in the dark. As he dug out the makings, she asked him what on earth he was doing. He said he meant to have a smoke. She protested that tobacco was against her religion. He said that was all right, he'd just smoke it himself, once he got it rolled.

She leaped out of bed, saying she was sure the hall was clear now, and was out the door, dragging her nightgown after her, before he could stop her. All he got to see of her was a pink flash before the door shut, plunging him into the dark again. He chuckled, finished rolling, and smoked until he felt sleepy again.

Willy the Death would surely know who'd brought him a late night snack, right?

CHAPTER
NINE

It didn't work. There was no way to ask at the breakfast table which one of the ladies present might have crept into bed with him the night before. Even the hired help acted as if butter wouldn't melt in their mouths. Only one of them looked chubby enough as she served the flapjacks. The pretty landlady at the head of the table looked too slender. Sister Bertha, across from him, looked a mite more qualified and didn't seem to want to meet his eye. On the other hand she acted shy with everyone, and didn't seem as well rounded as he fondly remembered. The trouble with that was that none of 'em looked, fully dressed, the way they might feel, and there was no way a man could steal even a little feel in mixed company.

After breakfast Stringer caught the chastized Willy the Death alone in the garden, weeding on his hands and knees. Stringer hunkered down beside him and yanked a sprouting chickweed as he said, "Don't look so glum, old pard. At least you got milk and a sandwich to sleep on, right?"

The kid scowled and said, "That'll be the day. When my mom sends me to bed with no supper, she means it, and as soon as I get big enough, I'm going to run off and join the Apache!"

Stringer said he felt sure the little rascal would make a fine Apache, and stood up with a puzzled frown. Then he shrugged and let himself out the gate, muttering, "Perfidity, thy name is woman."

He headed for the center of town, meaning to ask directions to the county courthouse. Then he spotted a newspaper establishment across the street and went over to see if he could save some time. Small-town newspapers only kept newsworthy items in their morgues. Pawing through dusty county records could get tedious unless one really cared about the births, deaths, marriages, and such of all sorts of uninteresting strangers.

As he entered, a bell above the door tinkled and an old gent wearing glasses and a smudge of printer's ink came out from the press room to ask what Stringer wanted. He looked disgusted to learn Stringer didn't want to place an ad, and dubious when Stringer told him who he was.

The old man said, "I have read and admired features written by Stringer MacKail. You can't be him. He writes literate."

Stringer smiled sheepishly and said, "I majored in writing, not oration. You talk sort of cow yourself, no offense, and I imagine you still spell most of the words right when you stick a galley."

The old man cocked an eyebrow at the newspaper jargon. Then he said, "My devil talks about cowboys too. I wish I knew where the hell he is this morning. Can you stick type, or are you just showing off, son?"

Stringer said, "The *Sun* uses union-set linotype these days, but I reckon I've worked on a few more modest papers in my time."

The old man said, "We'll see about that. Come on back and give me a hand. If you don't make too much pie, I might let you look through my morgue once we get this damned issue out."

Stringer followed him back to the press room. It was a typical small-town layout. There were Edison bulbs hanging above the work table, but the one press was an old hand-cranked antique. The old man handed Stringer a sheet of foolscap covered with handwriting or chicken tracks, depending on whether one held Palmer Penmanship in esteem, and said, "Stick this. Don't galley it until I see how you mind your P's and Q's."

Stringer hung up his hat and jacket, stepped over to the case table, and picked up an empty stick, muttering, "P's and Q's, for God's sake."

The partitioned wooden type trays, or cases, were set at a handy slant. Capital-letter type was stored in the harder-to-reach upper case. The more frequently used small letters were, of course, in the handier lower case. Stringer held the composing stick, which was really more like a flat metal box with a sliding margin block, in his left hand as he picked type with his right. Reading the handwritten copy, he stuck, not set, the type upside down and backward with the top line at the bottom of his stick. The old saw about P's and Q's derived from the simple fact that a lower-case P could be mistaken for Q, reading it backward, and vice versa. Stories about the notion deriving from Pints and Quarts or Peeps and Quacks had actually appeared in print, stuck by printers who surely should have known better.

The copy Stringer was sticking was a news item about a record head of lettuce grown by a local lady gardener with plenty of time, water, and the Arizona sun to work with. When he'd filled the stick, Stringer showed it to the old man, who'd been working on another item, of course. The old man examined his work, said, "Galley it," and added, grudgingly, "You can call me Tim, Stringer."

They got on even better after Stringer set, not stuck, the paragraph in the flat cast-iron frame, or galley, on a nearby table without spilling the type. As they worked side by side, old Tim was willing to talk more, now that he knew they were both old pros. Neither was distracted by discussing other subjects as they stuck from copy, because while both stuck at about the rate of a slow typist, reading that slow left plenty of time for thinking about other matters.

Stringer was glad he'd come, despite the ink he was getting on his left thumb because the missing devil was apparently a slob who broke type without cleaning it good before putting it back in the cases. Old Tim was a font of local information, and being an old-timer in the territory, remembered lots of things that might not have been in any morgue. Papers only kept what they'd once published, and a lot of details hadn't seemed important enough at the time.

By the time he'd helped the old man put the edition to bed, or had all the type bedded down in the galleys for the press to run off one at a time, he'd

learned more minor details of the Pleasant Valley
War and Sheriff Owens's career in general than Sam
Barca would have let him run, even if it had sounded
more interesting. Old Tim didn't make a liar out of
anyone he didn't already have down as a sneak. So
as they washed up with naptha and soft soap at a
corner sink, Stringer said, "Whether it was John
Tewskbury Junior or Indian John himself that got
shot on his way to the creek for water, seems less
important now than it might have years ago. The
point is that all the Tewksbury and Graham boys
wound up dead or scattered to parts unknown,
right?"

Old Tim shook his head and said, "Wrong. Old
Ed Tewksbury lives right here in Globe. Or he did
the last time I saw him. He's not just getting on in
years, he's been sick a spell."

Stringer started to ask which Tewksbury they were
talking about. Then he nodded and said, "You mean
the one they called Big Ed? I thought Sheriff Owens
arrested him years ago for murder."

The older man said, "He sure did. He was suspected of killing Tom Graham, among others. They
couldn't hold him up in Navajo County though. The
higher court held it was an unlawsome arrest. Owens
had no real jurisdiction over Pleasant Valley matters,
bad as they got. Big Ed knew better than to ever go
back there once they had to let him go. He did better
down this way, where he belonged. Served as a town
deputy a few years back as a matter of fact. Reckon
he reformed, whether he was a killer in his wild west
days or not."

Stringer whistled and asked if Jim had the old gun
slick's address. Old Tim said he didn't, but that it

would surely be in the city directory. He had one handy, and it was. As Stringer was writing it down he asked what old Tim might know about the mysterious Sol Barth. The old timer frowned, said he'd heard the name but couldn't place it, and asked if Stringer had time for a beer.

Stringer didn't. He'd spent close to three hours getting to know old Tim and this part of Arizona Territory better. So they parted friendly, and he legged it up to the current residence of Big Ed Tewksbury, assuming he was still there.

He was, seated on his porch in a rocker with a blanket over his lap, even though it was pushing high noon and felt like it. It was easy to see why he'd been called Big Ed in his day. He was a ruined giant with the features of his Indian mother and the rangy build of the Anglo-Saxon Indian John. Stringer introduced himself and told the sickly-looking old timer why he'd come to interview him, slanting the story some to avoid insulting an elder who'd once been tamed considerable by the true object of Sam Barca's esteem.

The last of the Tewksburys was soft spoken, friendly enough, and sort of embarrassed by his eventful past. He said, "I'd like to think we'd lived all that feuding and fussing down, son. It was our elders who started the feud in the first damn place, and anyone here in Globe can tell you I've lived decent and peaceful a good ten years or more. It's not true that me and Johnny Rhodes bushwacked the last of the Grahams. That tale about Tom Graham saying we was his killers as he lay dying was a spiteful lie, either by a man who hated ferocious enough to lie as he lay dying, or by an overly-eager sheriff who couldn't tell where county lines might run. Rhodes proved in open court he had a perfect alibi for the time they say Tom Graham was bushwacked. I didn't, I'll allow. But here I am. So let's say no more about it."

Stringer said soothingly, "I reckon a lot of the gossip both sides were subjected to must have vexed you some. Do you know a man in Saint John's called Sol Barth?"

Big Ed rocked back and forth as he gathered his memories together before he nodded and said, "Sure. Mexican Sol. Owned a general store, and just about everything else in Saint John's by the time he was through. Married into a big Mex family and sided with 'em against everyone else. What about him?"

Stringer said, "He says he's looking for me. Or, that is, he says I might know something about two gun slicks he used to have working for him."

Big Ed shot him a canny look and asked, "Since you say they was gun slicks, I don't reckon I want to know how come they ain't on his payroll no more. Was they Mex?"

Stringer shook his head and said, "Both Anglo. Both sort of old-timers as well."

Big Ed frowned and said, "That don't sound like Mexican Sol. I can't say for sure he's still in Saint John's. I ain't been up that way in years, and never spoke to the son of a bitch when I was there. He didn't have many Anglo pals. It was one of the few things me and even Pear Owens agreed on. Barth is, or was, a moody hard-to-get-along-with cuss."

"Was he an enemy of Sheriff Owens as well?"

"Enemy might be too strong a word. I know Pear warned Barth to keep his Mex friends in line, more than once. Whether we was picking on them or they was picking on us depends on who recalls what, from which dance that turned into a free-for-all. Owens had to save many a Mex from an Anglo lynch mob, and vice versa when they come after one of our boys with a rope. I don't recall Pear ever arresting Barth whilst the country up yonder was all one big county. It got quieter after Navajo County split off, with Holbrook as the county seat. I'd steer clear of Barth and old Saint John's if I was you, son. Both the town and old Barth is half Mex and unfriendly to strangers."

Stringer said, "I've been thinking about that. Unless he's inviting me to a showdown by public telegraph wire, he wired here crazy as hell. Do you know a deputy called Ed Nolan, Big Ed?"

The old timer chuckled and said, "Ed is a common name for deputies in these parts. Can't say Nolan means much to me. But it's been a spell since I packed a badge. What about him?"

"He says he doesn't know Sol Barth either. Yet Sol Barth wired him about me, by name, asking what I might know about his missing gun slicks. I know he only told Nolan they were hired hands. But he must have known, if I knew anything at all about them, I'd know he'd sent him after me. Does that make sense to you, sir?"

Big Ed Tewksbury said, "Nope, and I told you I didn't want to hear about any recent feuding. I told you Sol Barth had always had a rap for acting odd as hell. So go ask him, or better yet, stay the hell away from him."

Stringer said, "Saint John's is out of my way home, and I don't want to tire you, sir. So I'd like to ask you just one question about that range you once fought over, up in Pleasant Valley."

The sickly giant scowled up at him and snapped, "That war's been over for years. I've never been back. There's a curse on that land. The devil led us all into blood and slaughter up that way, and the devil is welcome to it all."

Stringer insisted, "Someone even meaner seems to be out to hog it, sir. You must have heard all the tales they tell about new settlers being driven off by haunts and worse. I'd like to hear a real Tewksbury offer an educated guess as to why things stayed so mysterious after both you and the Graham faction just packed it in and moved away."

The last of the Tewksburys shrugged and said, "Some of us just got sensible, I reckon. There's nothing up that way worth fighting that hard over. There never was. I'm ashamed to say now that it took both sides so long to see that. It ain't like Arizona is crowded, you know, even today. There's open range enough for one and all. None of it's worth spilling blood for. It don't rain all that much out here."

Stringer nodded and said, "I noticed how fast the chaparral moves in when you graze Arizona hard. You've been mighty helpful, and I thank you, sir. One more question. Do you still hold a title to the water rights up yonder?"

Big Ed looked startled, laughed, and said, "Hell, no. That's all federal land now. You could file on that water yourself, if you wanted to."

Stringer said, "I don't want to. Someone else doesn't seem to want anyone else to either."

So Big Ed asked, "Why don't he just claim it for himself, then?"

And Stringer said, "I don't know. I said it was crazy as hell."

Stringer was coming out of the feed store across from the livery when Deputy Nolan caught up with him again. The somberly dressed Nolan nodded at the big sack of oats on Stringer's left shoulder and said, "I see you're really going."

Stringer said, "I'm going north after sundown. First I got to go across the street and put this sack down. Unless they just cheated me, I've got forty pounds of oats here."

As they crossed to the shady side together, Stringer explained, "Now that I know the trail, I mean to travel mostly at night, with more speed, comfort, and supplies. I'll let you know if I see any haunts in the dark, or any candle stubs in mason jars if they get too close to me and mine."

Nolan followed him into the tack room. As Stringer dropped the feed sack at one end of the long wooden saddle horse, Ed Nolan said, "I hear you just paid a call on old man Tewksbury."

Stringer said, "I'd sure hate to have a secret vice in this old town. I'm not sure Big Ed is that old. But he sure looks sick as hell. Do you know what ails him?"

Nolan said, "Some say it's a bum ticker and others say it's a guilty conscience. Either way, the docs only give him a year or so more to live. What else did you two talk about?"

Stringer said, "Old wars and recent haunts, of course. He was unable to offer any sensible sugges-

tions. He said no survivors on either side had any
interest up that way now, and he pointed out another
odd thing. He pointed out that anyone who *wanted*
that abandoned range could have it free, off Uncle
Sam. It sort of makes one wonder why anyone would
run about acting loco in the *cabeza* when all he'd
have to do is fill out a few papers and pay a modest
filing fee to the land office."

Nolan nodded and said, "I've always said a man
would have to be loco to haunt a house a lot closer to
civilization. How do you put it all together, Mac-
Kail?"

Stringer said, "I just told you. I can't. I might
worry more about it if I was a lawman. But I doubt
I'll ever figure out how high *up* might go, or who
created the creator. Unsolved mysteries don't sell
newspapers, as my boss, Old Sam, keeps pointing
out to me every time I got bogged down on a story."

Nolan asked, "Then you're just giving up?"

Stringer said, "I just said that too. I should think
you boys who get *paid* to worry about sinister local
doings would show more interest in those haunts than
anyone has, up to now."

Nolan grimaced and said, "If I had a dollar for
every time I've poked around up that way, I'd buy
everyone a drink. Plenty of folk have filed complaints with Gila, and hell, Navajo and Coconino
counties. But nobody packing a badge has ever seen
a thing up there. We thought the first nesters chased
out by haunts were drunks. We still can't prove anyone's ever really seen or heard anything up that way.
Though it does seem odd their stories match, if they
were just making up excuses for not sticking out a
claim."

Stringer said, "The riders from the Hash Knife I ran into said they didn't believe in haunts either. You could be right. Some nesters hate to admit they just couldn't cut it with a nagging wife in a nagging climate. I know I can't wait to get back to the cool fogs of Frisco, and if you boys don't care, *I* don't care why some raving lunatic seems to want to preserve Pleasant Valley in a pure state of nature."

Nolan smiled thinly and said, "Maybe he thinks it looks more pleasant that way." Then he said, more seriously, "I don't know if I ought to tell you this—it being privileged information between us and the sheriff's department up to Saint John's—but as you mean to head north again, alone, I'd better tell you anyway."

Stringer waited. Nolan looked away and said, "We seem to have been slickered. That wire from Sol Barth was a fake. They say he ain't in business in Saint John's no more. They don't know where Barth, his Mex wife, and all their half-Mex kids went. But it's been some time since any of 'em was in a position to send wires from there. So who do you figure wired us about you and a couple of other mysterious travelers?"

Stringer said, "Someone who didn't want to sign his own name, of course. He knew Barth was known up that way, figured you might not check with the law, and may be waiting for a reply to that wire, still calling himself Sol Barth."

Nolan said, "We already thought of that. We got the Western Union office in Saint John's staked. So far he ain't showed. The fool kid clerk up there can't even describe the cuss who sent that wire for us.

How do you like the notion he was just trying to make trouble for you, MacKail?"

Stringer said, "Has he made any trouble for me, Ed?"

And Nolan replied, "Not as far as we can see. You're free to ride on out anytime you like. But if I was you, I'd take some pals with me. It's starting to look more and more like you got a lunatic showing considerable interest in you, MacKail."

Stringer hadn't checked into Prue Reynolds' boarding house with any luggage. So, tempting as her suppers were, he never went back there. At least one of her boarders was at least a mite odd, too, and he had enough to figure out in these parts.

He ate at a beanery, swore he'd never do that again, and made a few last calls to tie Globe up neat enough to forget as he left it. He rode out after sundown, riding the paint and leading the buckskin, this time packing more grub and less water. Remembering little Concepción with more than fondness, he reined in from time to time to study his back trail. But nobody seemed to be following him in the moonlight.

That left ambushes ahead. So when he got back to the mouth of Cherry Creek, with the sky pearling gray to the east again, he crossed over to the far side and holed up in some palo verde to let the sun and anyone else out to kill him figure out where he might be.

He didn't sleep all day. Nobody could have, even in the late-afternoon shade. He made himself wait, watering his ponies from time to time and reading all the notes Patty Stern had given him over and over, along with his own notes taken down in shorthand during his recent travels. He had more pieces of puzzle to work with than he likely needed, for try as he might, he couldn't get them all to fit just right. From time to time he'd come up with an almost good notion. Then he'd see there was no proof, or worse yet, other details that shot the notion full of holes.

He put all the fool paper away, grubbed himself good, smoked too much, and headed out again before the sun was all the way down, but at least a cooler shade of tomato red.

It wasn't so bad. That unseasonable rain they'd had was starting to show interesting results now. The chaparral looked greener, and the desert pavement between all but the poison-rooted creosote bushes was spangled with tiny little multicolored flowers that looked like miscrocopic daisies and would go to seed and die within days. A lot of desert flowers got by being seeds instead of anything more alive most of the time. As the shadows lengthened, critters who'd been hiding out were taking advantage of the modest green-out. Gaudy orange and black pelican bugs were feeding on fresh mesquite leaves. Nothing was feeding on them because they tasted awful, even to a lizard.

He spotted a big fat chuckwalla feeding on the little flowers. A baby dragon eating baby nosegays sure looked funny. He knew the snakes would soon be at their most dangerous time of day, so he stopped to swap horses in an open expanse of gray gravel, and it was still close, according to the skittish paint. He spotted the pretty little critter that had spooked her, peeking out from under some yucca, and calmed her down, soothing, "It ain't, Paint. Red next to black is all right, Jack. It's red next to yeller that can kill a feller. Haven't you ever seen a false coral snake before? They're a lot more common than the real thing, and hell, neither bother you much if you leave 'em alone."

He mounted up and rode on, knowing the heavier tread of his ponies would warn any snake that wasn't dead drunk that they were coming. Even the nasty desert diamondback fed on nothing larger than jack rabbit, and had no reason to strike at anything bigger, as long as it wasn't taken by surprise.

An hour or so later it was too cool to worry about snakes. The next time he stopped to water and swap, he dug out his sheepskin coat. It was even colder tonight than that gal back in Globe had complained about. The air was drier each night after a rain, and couldn't hold as much heat after sundown.

He stared up at the cold, black star-spangled sky to make sure of his bearings as he cut through the chaparral where no trails ran. His plan was to follow the western rather than eastern high ground this time. He had two reasons. He knew he might spot something looking east that he'd missed looking west, and he knew anyone laying for him would expect him to take the same trail back.

They made good time once they found another deer trail and rode along it at a trot now and again, where it was easy to see. He had to keep warning himself not to let his guard down as mile after mile passed under him with no sign of trouble. He holed up again at dawn amid a nest of boulders topped by mesquite aspiring to be real trees instead of glorified bushes. Things went as well all the way to the head of Pleasant Valley, and as he made camp that one last morning, the view down there looked pleasant as hell.

The grass was still yellow, save at the roots, of course, but the whole valley was now an oriental carpet of tawny grass, golden poppies, and purple desert lupine. Here and again a clump of cottonwood or willow rose from the rug to brag about all the water at their roots. The creek itself was now running low, and it's bed was braided with lots of exposed sand. But there was still enough running water to glitter like fool's gold in the dawn's slanting sunlight. Stringer was sitting with his back to a boulder, enjoying the view as he rolled a smoke, when he heard hoof steps coming up the slope behind him and spun to his feet, .38 in hand.

He saw it was a shabby little gent on foot, leading a heavily laden burro. The old timer waved at him and called out, "Howdy. I don't suppose you have any coffee to spare."

Stringer called back, "No, but I'll share with you anyways. Where in hell have you come from with that poor jackass?"

The old timer pointed back at the distant Ancha hills dividing this basin from the Tonto, and replied, "She's a jenny. My name is Mo Glass, and I've come from Prescott, bound for the Zuni pueblos to the east."

Stringer said, "You must like to walk a lot, cutting across the grain like so."

As he tethered his burro near Stringer's ponies and broke out a nose bag to water her, old Mo said, "I hate walking. But I'm an Indian trader, and I can't get the savage bastards to live near railroad tracks. This may be the hard way, but it's still the short way. I know because I have to torture myself this way all the time."

As they hunkered down by Stringer's pot, waiting for it to come to a boil, the old trader told him his simple story. He was headquartered in Prescott, where he could order shipments by rail and from whence his wife refused to stir whether he was there or not. He confided that he had a Zuni gal farther east, and that it served his white woman right. The Indians had learned to trust him over the years. So they depended on him for German coal-tar dies for their blankets, abalone shell and cinnabar for their coin-silver jewelry, and patent medicines for what ailed them. He confided, "My Zuni gal is the daughter of a medicine man. He don't let on, but you'd be surprised how much of them new aspirin powders he mixes in with his feather shaking. On my way back I'll be loaded up with mighty fine silver work. In my opinion Zuni work has that gaudy Navajo crap beat hollow. I ain't as easy about hailing strangers when I'm packing silver. But you don't have to shoot me if you want some aspirin or coal-tar colors."

Stringer said he hardly ever murdered his elders, and added, "I've heard the same can't be said for others in these parts. Do you come through Pleasant Valley often, Mo?"

The old man nodded down at the fine view and said, "Just to cross it. I water at the old abandoned homestead down among them willows. Why do you ask?"

Stringer answered, "I've been told the Tewksbury who once lived there was picked off carrying water a much shorter distance. Yet you say you've never had any trouble down yonder?"

Old Mo nodded and said, "Hardly ever meet anyone this far from all over. I meet a young hand like you, out after strays or whatever, now and again. None of you have ever throwed me down and robbed me of my virtue, or even aspirin powders. I hope you don't have someone gunning for you, son, for if you do, I'll just be on my way and you can drink all your coffee. I'm a a man with a better head for business than fighting."

Stringer said, "Simmer down, Mo. I don't think anyone is out to gun anyone this morning. I did have some trouble going the other way a few days ago. Now nobody seems interested, and you say they let you pass through regular. If I could figure that out, I wouldn't feel so dumb."

As they shared Stringer's coffee and some interesting salami from old Mo's pack, he brought the old-timer up on his recent adventures. The old timer agreed it was a poser. He said, "I've often wondered how come nobody ever saw fit to reclaim this range. That's not my line. But even I can see it's a handsome spot for a homestead, and you should see some of the dumb places to homestead I've passed in my travels across this dusty land. We heard a little in Prescott about the range wars over this way. But I thought they'd been settled years ago."

Stringer said, "They were. All the participants are long gone. But though others have tried to move in, they've all been driven out, like I told you."

The canny old trader said, "Try it this way. With nobody living within miles, your mastermind can't be guarding it all the time. He just checks from time to time, or hell, he can get it at the land office whenever someone means to settle anywhere down there long enough to matter."

Stringer stared at the old man in admiration and said, "That works. That's why gents like you and Hash Knife riders aren't bothered when you pass this way. The mastermind neither knows nor cares about casual visitors."

Old Mo said, "Hold on. We may not be so smart after all. You didn't file any claims at any land office, did you, son?"

Stringer said, "No. I didn't even come out here to do a story on the damned old range. But let's try another tack. What if all this time they've been after me not to keep me from lookin down at all that grass, but because they're afraid I might discover yet another dirty secret they're trying to hide?"

Old Mo sipped more coffee, commented on how fine it tasted after two whole days without, and decided, "You say they tried to get you smack in town. Yep, if *I* wanted a man gunned, and he just refused to stay in town, I reckon I'd just try to have him gunned anywhere I could get at him."

"What about those Mexican cow thieves?" Stringer asked.

The old man laughed bitterly, and said, "Let's not get into racial prejudice. When a man hires his gun hand out to kill total strangers for pay, who's to say who he might kill free when he sees the chance? I don't think we're talking about nice people, son."

Stringer nodded and said, "Yeah, old Ed Tewksbury told me there was still some hard feelings between Anglos and Mexicans in these parts. The last of the gang I met up with was a mean old buzzard with the look of a natural killer. That Mex gal I told you about might have gotten more direct revenge than we thought at the time."

Old Mo finished his coffee, put the tin cup aside with a sigh, and got to his feet, saying, "That was grand, and I'm much obliged. But I have to get going."

"With the sun coming up instead of going down, Mo?"

The old man nodded firmly, and said, "Heat doesn't bother me as much as bullets. I like you, son. You seem like a decent young cuss. But, no offense, you seem to draw trouble like a turd draws flies, and whatever you're mixed up in, it ain't my fight."

Stringer didn't argue or blame him as old Mo repacked the nose bag, untethered his burro, and headed down the slope, not looking back. Stringer could watch them turning to smaller and smaller dots for a long time. He watched the old man fill his canteens at the creek down below. Then he watched them trudge on into the shimmering heat waves until he couldn't make them out anymore. He walked around his day camp, peering off in all directions until he was sure he had this high spot on the ridge to himself. Then he found some shade, covered his face with his hat, and tried to catch some shut-eye. He wasn't really sleep, but he knew he'd have to keep his wits about him from here on back to Holbrook. For if they ever meant to stop him out here, where only the gun was law, it would be soon. The Mogollon Rim would be a hell of a place to lay for a man, if you knew he was coming. There were lots of folk in Globe. He'd told lots of 'em where he was going too. If even one was a pal of the mastermind, they had to know he was coming.

CHAPTER
TEN

Apparently they didn't. Stringer might have made even better time if he hadn't had to scout so many grand ambush sites before passing them on his way back to Holbrook.

The sun caught him outside of town when it rose again. He rode in anyway. It was just starting to get good and hot by the time he reined in at the livery, dismounted with a weary sight, and led the brutes inside.

The livery man looked surprised, and said, "I was beginning to fear we'd never see you or them ponies again."

Stringer said, "I was worried about that a time or two. But here we are."

Stringer was free to leave with just his gladstone and the rifle. He knew he could get a decent price for a Krag on Mission Street, back in Frisco.

If it hadn't been so hot he might have been tempted to pay a call on old Madge first. But as in the case of that sneaky gal in Globe, there were all-too-rare times a man got a chance to quit while he was ahead, so there was no sense of tempting fate.

The Bucket of Blood Saloon was closer anyway. The beer was still warm, but had tepid canteen water beat. As he'd hoped, a couple of the early customers knew more about the comings and goings of the Santa Fe than he had before he talked to them.

Stringer was about to leave when Nate, the town law, came in for a cool-off. He joined Stringer at the bar and asked if the long ride to Globe and back had been worth it.

Stringer didn't kiss and tell. So he said, "It was more hot and tedious than educational. Am I square with the law here?"

Nate said, "Sure, unless you kilt someone else since that last coroner's jury cleared you. Why? You planned on going someplace else?"

Stringer nodded and said, "I have to. I don't live around here. I'm hoping to catch the westbound that passes through here just after noonday. First I have to go settle accounts with Lawyer Addams. I don't think I owe him any money, but I only skip out on bills when I have to."

Nate said that sounded honest enough. Then Stringer asked him, "Could you rightly say how that gal, Patty Stern, got to be a widow woman? I don't want to ask her personal when I go over to their office."

Nate nodded and said, "That could upset her. They say it was a good marriage. He was only killed a year or so back. A lunatic client shot him, right in his office. As we put it together from the notes Lawyer Stern had been taking down as they talked alone up there, the client was an old geezer who was having trouble with a young wife. His vexation was sort of disjointed, and the lawyer had crossed things out and made him start over a time or two. This must have upset him, for he shot Stern considerable and lit out to find another lawyer or whatever. By the time anyone in the street who'd heard the gunfire could connect it to the wild-eyed rascal mounting up out front, he was long gone."

Nate inhaled some of his own suds before he added, "It's a good thing lawyer Addams was in court and Stern's young wife was at the beauty shop that afternoon. The lunatic might have gunned them too. He was a mean old son of a bitch."

Stringer asked, "Did anyone who saw him say what he might have looked like?"

Nate said, "They did. He was a grizzled geezer dressed shabby and wearing a beard. Why do you ask, at this late date?"

Stringer said, "I thought I might have seen him one time. What do you know about a merchant called Sol Barth, over to Saint John's?"

Nate grimaced and said, "Nothing good. He was said to be an ugly cuss who married a pretty young Mex gal and got upset as hell when anyone calt her a greaser. I'm speaking of events before my time though. Old Barth ain't in Saint John's these days, even though the odor of his gun smoke lingers on. Say, you ain't suggesting Sol Barth had something to do with the gunning of Patty Stern's man, are you?"

Stringer shook his head and said, "No. Someone else is trying to gun me. It's been nice talking to you, Nate. But I want to settle up at the law office before that train pulls in."

A few minutes later he was saying much the same

to the young blonde herself. She looked like the heat was getting her down, but she managed a wan smile as she told him Lawyer Addams would be back any minute, but that she was sure neither Stringer nor the *San Francisco Sun* owed them any money now.

He sat down anyway, resisting the desire to ask her permit to smoke, and said, "As long as I got time before my train gets here, I may as well go on being nosy. I don't want to stir up hurtful memories, Patty, but could I ask a few questions about your late husband?"

She looked more surprised than hurt as she nodded and said, "It doesn't hurt as much now as it did then. He was murdered by a client right in the next room, and—"

"I know about that," he cut in. Then he said, "Lawyer Addams mentioned riding posse under Sheriff Owens a time or two. Your man would have had to be younger at the time, unless you admire distinguished older gents, right?"

She nodded and said, "My man was only seven or eight years older than me, and as a matter of fact, he did some riding for the law in his younger days as well. Before we were married though. Why do you ask?"

He said, "Just trying to separate the sheep from the goats. I don't suppose he ever told you whether he'd ridden under Sheriff Owens during the troubles down Pleasant Valley way?"

She smiled wistfully and said, "You're wrong. You men folk tend to tell us woman folk more tales of blood and slaughter than we really want to hear, and he was all man. I guess it was the most exciting time of his life, riding posse as he was just starting up as a young lawyer. Before that stupid feud down there was over, he'd ridden all over that dark and bloody ground for the law."

"More than his pard, Lawyer Addams? I've a reason for asking."

She supressed a smile and said, "Well, we are talking about an older man who would have been sort of soft and pudgy, even ten years ago. I can't tell you just when, where, or how often he rode for Sheriff Owens though."

Stringer smiled crookedly and said, "That's all right. I can. Since the war with Spain I've met so many men as charged up San Juan Hill, it's a wonder one hill could hold them all. Not putting any man down, I feel it's safe to assume your late husband might have known Pleasant Valley better than his partner. I don't think he was killed by a lunatic client. I think he was killed to make sure he could never mention something he might have noticed in his travels to the south. If it's any comfort to you, I can almost assure you certain that the hired gun who murdered your man is dead and buzzard buried where he'll never be missed."

She gasped and began to demand an explanation. Then Lawyer Addams came in and she told him instead, "Mister MacKail, here, just said my man was murdered!" And then she began to cry.

Lawyer Addams waved Stringer into the room next door, and as soon as they were alone, he said, "That was uncalled for, MacKail. She's just about gotten over that tragedy, and now look what you have gone and done! What are you talking about anyway?"

Stringer said, "Murder. A gent who knew both the

law and the disputed Pleasant Valley range. I think he was killed by the same rascals who tried to keep me from tripping over their secret plans more recent. They might have figured I was more educated than the folk they've been content to flimflam with spook lights and such. I don't think it's a big gang, and it's been whittled down some. But the brains behind it all belongs to someone crazy-mean as well as slick."

Lawyer Addams said, "Well, let's hear what you've found out, for God's sake. If you have any charges to make, you ought to be going to the law with them, not upsetting poor Patty with wild talk!"

Stringer sighed and said, "I would, if I could prove anything, or hell, if I *knew* anything for certain. But as I told a gent named Nolan, down in Globe, I'm a newspaper man, not a lawyer. So I'm allowed to give up when I get confused. Riding alone the past few days, I've had plenty of time to think. So all in all I think my best bet is the next train out. It's no skin off my nose if the folk around here are dumb enough to let themselves get skinned. Is there another way out of here? I hate to say good-bye to weeping she-males."

Addams showed him to a side door leading out to the hall as he muttered, "I wish you'd at least tell me who you suspect of what, damn it. It's easy for you to just give up and head back to Frisco. Patty and me have to stay here, and if there's any danger to either of us—"

But Stringer stepped out into the hallway, saying, "I wouldn't be willing to drop it if I thought anyone here was likely to be gunned at this late date. I said I wasn't a lawman, but I'm not that irresponsible. The mastermind is crazy-mean, but not crazy enough to have anyone gunned who doesn't know what he's out to pull off in, oh, two or three years."

"Do you know who this mysterious mastermind might be?" asked the pudgy lawyer.

Stringer shook his head and said, "If I did, I'd have to tell the law. Then I'd get to print it in the *Sun*. I have plenty of suspects. Too many. I might work it out better once I get back to Frisco. I have a pal there who runs the big Western Union office on Market Street. Some night when it isn't too busy we may do some hunting by wire."

"Do what?" asked Addams with a puzzled frown.

Stringer explained, "My boss, Sam Barca, traced your old pal Commodore Perry Owens to Seligman without getting up from his desk. We got telephones at the *Sun* these days. I confess the rascals didn't leave me much sign to read on any trail I rode aboard a pony. But sometimes paper trails are easier to read. I know, for openers, that Western Union has to have records of a mess of flimflam telegrams that seem to have been sent to confuse me more. I shudder to think what they had planned if they'd been able to lure me to yet another out-of-the-way place with fibs about folk who don't live there no more. But it didn't work, and it's been nice talking to you, for I don't mean to miss that train if I can help it."

They shook, and Stringer went downstairs alone, gladstone in hand and rifle in the other. It was, in fact, too early to stand on the station platform in the glaring sunlight. So he had some pie at the beanery across from the depot and washed it down with buttermilk to settle his butterflies.

Then he checked the time, nodded, and drifted over to wait on the platform alone. He put his bag down, started to lean the Army rifle on it, then decided to hold it cradled casually across one elbow as he paced up and down the sun-baked planks.

He'd just turned at one end of the platform when he saw the somberly dressed Ed Nolan from Globe down at the other end, headed his way with a curious smile. Nolan's frock coat was open, which was reasonable in this heat, but he was wearing a buscadero gun rig under it. So before the son of a bitch was within easy pistol range, Stringer swung the muzzle of the Krag up and put a .30-30 rifle round in his chest.

As Nolan's hat flew straight up and Nolan flew straight back to crash, sprawling, on the planks, Stringer cranked another round in the Krag's chamber and approached the downed gun slick warily. Then he hunkered down by Nolan and said conversationally, "I figured you might ride up ahead of me. You had a good four or five hours lead. After we talked at the livery in Globe, I took the trouble to wire Saint John's, and guess what—nobody, by any name whatever, ever wired anybody anything about me, or Warner, or Coleman. On the other hand, the Western Union clerk in Globe said a man answering to your description wired Holbrook regular. They wouldn't let me read your messages, of course. But they would have been in code in any case, right?"

The dying Nolan didn't answer. He was blowing little red bubbles as he stared up at Stringer in hurt wonder. Stringer told him, "The reason I didn't screw around with a professional killer just now was that I knew your intent the moment I saw you'd dropped your deputy act. Anyone can say he's a deputy. But it starts to wear thin when you stretch it across two counties after lying outright to a gent as smart as me."

Then he saw that Nolan wasn't staring up at him, but at something behind him, with a sort of hopeful expression. So Stringer spun on one heel, fired the rifle up at Lawyer Addams, and rose to his feet without it, drawing his .38 as the fat bastard went down, too, squealing like a stuck pig, which was only to be expected when one considered where he'd been stuck by a .30-30.

Both men he'd downed were dead by the time the town law got there at the head of a considerable pack. Stringer holstered his revolver and kept his hands polite as he called out, "Hold your fire, Nate. It's over."

Nate said, "The hell you say! Who's this gent in the black suit, and how come you shot Lawyer Addams?"

Stringer said, "I had to shoot Nolan, there, because he was sent to gun me. I had to shoot Addams because Nolan was no doubt his last hired gun. I know that derringer in his pudgy hand looks sissy, but Lincoln was shot in the back of the head with the same kind of pistol, and I didn't want to see what it felt like."

Nate said, "You can forget about that next train, Stringer. No offense, but I fear you've got a lot of explaining to do!"

Stringer nodded and said, "That's all right. Explaining it all to the coroner saves me having to orate about it out here in this hot sun. The tale is sort of complicated."

CHAPTER
ELEVEN

The coroner's jury met at sundown, same place and same members, save for Lawyer Addams, whose unexpected demise was the subject of the inquest.

Patty Stern was there with other curious onlookers, more than one of whom seemed to feel an inquest was a needless formality, and that they ought to just string up the killer of their old pal, Lawyer Addams, right on the spot.

Patty sat sort of stone-faced in a corner and avoided Stringer's eye when he took his seat in front of the hard-eyed older men. Even the old judge who'd fallen asleep in his chair the last time was wide awake. The same coroner banged for silence with the butt of his six-gun and told Stringer, "We're ready to hear your side now, and it had better be good."

Stringer nodded, but said, "It was pure evil in the heart of one greedy man who, as a lawyer, got to meet lots of others who were willing to work cheap at being bad."

The coroner said, "We already wired Globe about the one called Nolan, and we know he was a fake deputy with no visible means of support and over a hundred dollars in his wallet. Get to the infernal point."

Stringer said, "I'm trying to. I said it was complicated. But to begin with, years ago a mess of contrary folk moved into the well named Pleasant Valley. As you know, they were too far from Globe and mayhaps too mean for Gila County to worry about. They were outside this county's jurisdication until a fine old sheriff who thought simple justice was more important than such petty details put an end to their outlaw notions of land ownership by showing both sides just how rough gun-law could get."

"We know all that. It was years ago, damn it."

"Hear me out. Sheriff Owens was just a good old boy out to clean up a mess. He may or may not have noticed what a fine range the Tewksbury clan and the Graham faction were fighting over. But he was a lawman, not a rancher, and in any case the valley lay outside his own home range. So he was only interested in stopping the bloodshed."

An old-timer down at the end of the table cackled, "That he done, although blood flowed like water by the time old Pear had things tamed."

Stringer nodded and said, "He didn't do it all alone. It would have been pure suicide. So, brave as he was, Owens had deputies backing his play. One was a young lawyer named Stern."

A panel member said, "Addams rid with them a time or two as well."

Stringer said, "Maybe not as often. But it doesn't really matter which lawyer noticed first what less educated members of the posses might not have. Both warring factions were holding overlapping claims on good range, by guts and guns instead of iron-bound legal papers. I don't think young Stern ever planned to grab the spoils himself. He never tried, when he still had the chance. But he must have noticed, and no doubt brought it to his partner's attention, that with both the Grahams and Tewksburys gone, all that land and the more important water rights lay fallow. There's been a lot of talk about irrigation projects down along the Salt River. At some future date any man who holds the water rights to the sources of Cherry Creek will be, or would be, in a position to write his own ticket. We're talking about an all-year stream in a land where water runs expensive."

Another panel member said, "As I follow your drift, you claim the late Lawyer Addams was a water-hogging land-grabber. Before I'll buy that you'll have to show me why he didn't just grab the durned old valley years ago, the minute it was empty."

Stringer said, "He couldn't. The claims were conflicting about the range. But each family settled there had at least filed a homestead claim. Land and water rights have to be abandoned seven years before they revert to public domain. Had Addams tried to file while the titles were still clouded, he'd have risked more publicity than he wanted, even if he'd been able to get away with it. He meant to wait until the upper valley was free and clear to claim before he claimed it all, using dummy claimants, to grab every quarter section at once, of course."

The coroner said, "We know how cattle barons get

title to free government land and water. Your sense of timing is still way off, son. Tom Graham was murdered ten or twelve years ago, not seven, and if he wasn't the last original claimant, I don't see who was."

Stringer chuckled dryly and said, "That's because you haven't been paying attention outside your own county line. It's all too true that one has to consider the Graham claims to any part of the valley abandoned, from the date Tom Graham was murdered by a person or person's unknown."

Someone growled, "Unknown, hell. It was Johnny Rhodes and Big Ed Tewksbury. Pear Owens arrested the rascals for that killing."

Stringer said, "I just paid a visit on Big Tewksbury down in Globe. He tells a different story. It's just as likely the last of the Grahams was gunned when he came back, less than seven years after Owens ran him off, by someone who didn't want him to prove his claim to all that water. But be that as it may, the same last Tewksbury told me his side had given up on the grass and water Addams wanted. Addams was a patient man. But it must have vexed him when, as one parcel of the valley after another reverted to public domain, new settlers started moving in to file on it."

Someone asked, "Why didn't he just file on it first?"

And Stringer said, "I told you. He wanted to grab it all at once. Had anyone as important as Addams showed interest in just one part of the valley, other locals, smarter than the half-baked greenhorns moving in from the south, might have wondered why, and he'd already had one law partner murdered to

keep the news from getting out. I agree it was complicated and sneaky. But I'd not have had to gun him
this afternoon if he hadn't been a complicated and
sneaky cuss. A more honest and sensible man would
have done it as you say, and been content to share
with others. But Addams was a natural hog. He
drove the settlers out as fast as they moved in. But,
of course, each time he did he was stuck with the fact
that each *new* claim had its proving time to run before he could grab it as public land. I know of at least
one little gal in Globe who still holds lawful title to
the springs at the head of the valley. I sort of hope
she's the gal I hope she might be. But to get back to
Addams, he was getting as confused as the folk he
was trying to flimflam by the time I showed up. I
know I said I was here to do a story on old Sheriff
Owens. I was. But being a double-dealing compul-
sive liar, Addams figured I had to be up to something
else. He knew Owens was now far away in another
county. He figured I was just playing dumb instead
of working for a dumb boss. He figured, as I was a
reporter known to do exposes on crooked doings, I'd
come here to dig up some secret I wasn't letting on
about. He knew, as a lawyer, that nobody in the
county was up to anything all that crooked but himself. So he put two and two together, came up with
five or six, and tried to run me or gun me before I
could say bad things about him in my paper. When I
licked his hired gun, Blue Streak Bendix, he knew I
took my job serious. So he had Blue Streak murdered
and forgot about running me. I was marked for
death, lest I tell the world he was trying to become a
water baron by behaving so ornery to anyone who
even looked serious at the water rights to the south."

The old judge frowned at him and said, "Hold on now, son. As I recall, you was defended in this very room by the law firm of Stern and Addams. You got off too."

Stringer nodded and said, "I reckon we'd best call it Stern and Stern, now. He murdered one Stern, but the other one still works there, and now, likely owns the whole shebang. He had to act the part of my lawyer when I went to him for help. I told you he was sneaky. He had to do a good job for me because Miss Patty got to do all the paper work, and she wasn't in on anything crooked with him. Throwing me to the wolves wouldn't have worked in any case. No offense, but had you bound me over to your grand jury, my boss would have sent other lawyers, and Addams knew for sure I wasn't guilty."

An old panel member who hadn't spoken until now sighed and said, "We was smart enough to see you couldn't have killed Blue Streak that time. Get to the good parts, damn it."

Stringer said, "There's not much more to it. Whoever first said honesty was the best policy knew what he was talking about. I never would have stumbled into the tangled web a natural cheat had woven if they'd simply left me alone. But they wouldn't. So I kept floundering around, and they kept trying to kill me or slicker me, until Addams had his hired gun, Nolan, scout me up down in Globe. I don't know what his original orders were, but when he questioned me and discovered how dumb I really was, they must have changed plans. The whole scheme was to keep Pleasant Valley quiet and pleasant, not littered with corpses, until Addams could make a quick grab for all of it at once. Instead of laying for me on the trail as I rode back, Nolan rode on ahead to report in for further duties. He may have been their top gun. I know he was cooler than some of the earlier ones I met. Anyway, I think they meant to let me get away, secure in the belief I had, indeed, just been a nosy stranger who hadn't been so smart after all. As I parted company with Addams I let it slip, deliberate, that I had a few irons left in the fire after all, including the fact that their flimflam with telegrams never sent had been a dumb notion."

"What first put you on to that?" asked the coroner.

The weary Stringer replied, "I knew right off it had to be a lie, unless it was dumb as hell. Whether the real Sol Barth had been the mastermind or not, he'd have never signed his own name to a wire showing guilty knowledge. I couldn't see anyone else using the name of a well-known big shot in a tiny town. I wasn't too surprised to learn, easy enough, no such wire had ever been sent. Knowing Nolan had approached me with one lie, it was easy enough to ask a few gents in Globe if they had a deputy there named Ed Nolan. When I saw him here in Holbrook this afternoon, I knew there was just no way he could have *followed* me from Globe. I was watching for that, as well as making good time. So I shot him."

There was a moment of stunned silence. Then the coroner asked, "Just like that? With no real proof?"

Stringer nodded soberly and said, "A man can wind up dead, asking a professional killer to confess, when he's coming at one with an innocent smile and a tie-down holster. I'll allow that could be taken as a mite hasty on my part. But I knew for sure I'd been right when Lawyer Addams moved in to shoot me in the back. The record will note *his* gun was already in his hand when I shot *him*. He'd have hardly come at me that way if he'd been a lawyer who'd just seen a known client win a fight with a stranger. So it's safe to assume Nolan was no stranger to Addams and that his actions were those of an outraged employer who'd just lost his last good gun slick."

The coroner asked if he was finished. Stringer nodded and said he couldn't think of anything important he wanted to add to his testimony.

The coroner stared morosely at him and said, "I don't know, son. Your story sounds convincing, but it's still just your say-so against gents in no position to call you a big fibber. Can't you produce any material evidence at all to back any part of your complicated reading of a dead man's mind?"

Stringer couldn't. So he didn't answer.

Then Patty Stern stood up in the corner to call out, "I may be able to." They all stared in her in wonder as she came forward with a sheaf of carbon papers in her hands.

She placed them on the table before the coroner and explained, "I got these from the office files when I heard about this hearing. I frankly didn't know what they might mean until just now. I dug them out because they were the only papers I'd ever been asked to file that, to me, made little sense. I remember asking my late husband's partner why we kept getting these carbons from the federal land office, since none of the names seemed to be clients or even anyone I knew. He acted a bit vague about it and said he'd explain later. But he never did. They didn't seem important, so I didn't argue. I just put them away as he asked. Now that I've heard Stuart

MacKail's testimony, I think I see why a law firm in Navajo County was keeping tabs on homestead claims in Gila County."

The coroner started leafing through the carbons, passing some on to his jurors. As the rustic but smart old gents examined the evidence, there were low growls directed at the memory of the late Lawyer Addams. The coroner nodded, banged for silence, and said, "This stuff's material enough, I reckon. I find that if that fat, dead son of a bitch hadn't been mighty interested in the water rights of Pleasant Valley, he'd have had no call to request copies of every claim filed down that way, dating way the hell back. So I further find that young McKail, here, was acting in self-defense, and it's too bad he didn't gut-shoot both the sneaky rascals!"

There was a general murmur of agreement and mention of the saloon next door. Stringer got to his feet, too, but didn't join the mad stampede for the Bucket of Blood. He waited quietly until Patty Stern joined him, her eyes glowing up at him sort of friendly as she said, "Oh, Stuart, how can I ever thank you?"

He said, "You were the one who saved my hash, so I get to thank you harder. Can I walk you home?"

She said, "You'd better. My knees feel a little weak. I didn't fully realize the burden I'd been carrying all this time, until you lifted it from me today."

As he helped her down the stairs he asked if she meant old Addams had been more than fatherly to her since her husband had left him the whole business.

She said, "Oh, not at all. I thought he was very kind, until you exposed him for what he was. Do you think he'd have had me murdered, too, if he thought I knew anything?"

Stringer said, "Yep. He may have kept you on as his filing gal so he could keep an eye on you and make sure you stayed as dumb as he wanted. But now the firm is all yours, and you can surely hire an honest young lawyer to argue in court for you until Arizona gets less stuffy."

She said, "That's not what I meant, although I guess I owe you for that too. You see, until you told me my husband had been the victim of a premeditated murder, I couldn't help feeling I was at least partly responsible for his death."

He took her arm to steady her as they walked the plank sidewalk, and told her, "That was dumb. You had nothing to do with it, did you?"

She said, "I know it wasn't rational. But we all thought it was the work of a lunatic, and I couldn't help thinking that if I'd been at the reception desk instead of having my hair done that awful afternoon—"

"You've have been murdered too," he cut in, adding, "Addams didn't like you *that* much."

She said, "I know. I just said you'd lifted a terrible burden of guilt from my shoulders. I can face what happened calmly now. I loved him. But he's gone, through no fault of my own, and life must go on."

At the next corner she indicated a turn up a side street that was more a glorified lane. As they moved up it, arm in arm, she asked what his plans were, now that he'd solved the mystery of the haunted range.

He said, "For openers I have to get it down on

paper. I'm sure they'll give me two columns at space rates for a wild west yarn as wild as this one turned out."

She reined him in by the garden gate of a little poplar-shaded cottage, and said with a sigh, "I'm afraid this is where I live. I guess you're sort of anxious to get back to San Francisco now, huh?"

He said, "That's where my typewriter lives. Even if I had one here in Holbrook, I somehow doubt I'd get much typing done at that Majestic Hotel."

She nodded and said, "I told you that old Harvey Girl runs a disorderly place. But finding you a typewriter would be no bother. There are three of them at the office, and thanks to you they're all mine now."

He said, "That's a mighty neighborly offer. But while I can type up my feature just as good in one place as another, can you give me one good reason why I might want to do it here instead of back in Frisco?"

She stared up at him sort of dreamy-eyed in the moonlight as she slowly opened her gate and said, "You'd better come on in with me so we can discuss the matter in more depth."